The Pumpkin Murders

The Pumpkin Murders

Judith Alguire

Doug Whiteway, Editor

Signature
EDITIONS

Cover design by Doowah Design.
Photo of Judith Alguire by Taylor Studios, Kingston.

This book was printed on Ancient Forest Friendly paper.
Printed and bound in Canada by Marquis Book Printing Inc.

We acknowledge the support of the Canada Council for the Arts and the Manitoba Arts Council for our publishing program.

Library and Archives Canada Cataloguing in Publication

Alguire, Judith
          The pumpkin murders / Judith Alguire.

ISBN 978-1-897109-45-8

          I. Title.

PS8551.L477P86 2010   C813'.54   C2010-905616-7

Signature Editions
P.O. Box 206, RPO Corydon, Winnipeg, Manitoba, R3M 3S7
www.signature-editions.com

To Sadie, Newt, and Gus the Bus

Chapter One

"Where are you going?" Adolph came out of the kitchen carrying a plate and a tea towel. He was wearing a gingham apron that fell to his ankles.

Gerald zipped up his jacket. "I think I left my wallet at work."

"Won't it be safe until tomorrow?"

Gerald paused in front of the hall mirror to fluff his hair. "Surely you jest. Some of those people would steal pennies off the eyes of their dead grandmothers." He hesitated. "I don't suppose you have money for a cab."

"I'll lend you bus fare." Adolph reached into his pocket and pulled out a handful of change.

Gerald gave him an aggrieved look but took the money. "Imagine, reduced to taking a bus."

"It's been done, Gerald."

Gerald gave the mirror a final look. "If I'm not back by midnight, give my clothes to Hector." He dashed out, slamming the door behind him.

Adolph stood, absently drying the plate and listening to the diminishing clatter of Gerald's shoes on the stairs. Finally, he returned to the kitchen, stacked the plate in the cupboard, removed his apron, and hung it on a hook beside the door.

He told himself he never should have let Gerald move in. He had known him for several years and was aware of his proclivities.

But Gerald had begged and he couldn't say no. Why? Because he was spineless. He brushed a strand of wispy sandy hair from his forehead. Because he was lonely. Because life seemed humdrum.

He took off his glasses, polished them, set them back on his nose. One ear was higher than the other. The asymmetry had distorted the frames over the years. Gerald would never commit such a fashion faux pas. Gerald would have his ears surgically altered.

He glanced into Gerald's room as he passed into the living room. As meticulous as Gerald was about his appearance, he was a disaster around the apartment. Left things where he dropped them. Never lifted a finger to help with the housekeeping. Seemed to think food found its way to the table on its own.

Adolph sank into his chair, absorbing the silence. Because Gerald brought an excitement to the apartment that made him feel more alive than he had in his previous thirty-eight years. Having Gerald around was like replacing a forty-watt bulb with a floodlight.

"I should have loaned him the money for the cab," he said to himself. "What's another twenty dollars?"

Gerald left the bus as gracefully as possible, given that he had to squeeze past a woman carrying several bags and a man with a belly that extended halfway across the aisle. Talk about your smelly masses, he thought. He made a beeline to the corner and turned into a side street. Halfway down, he stopped in front of a long, one-storey building with boarded windows. He slipped into the alley that ran alongside the building, counting the windows until he found the one he frequently popped open for a smoke. He jiggled the window up and crawled through, leaving it open. "Now where, Gerald?" he muttered to himself, tapping an index finger against his lips. If he'd left the wallet here, the most logical place to look would be the dressing room.

He sniffed. Not a formal dressing room, mind you, the sort you'd find in the better places. Just an eight-by-ten with a spotty mirror, a couple of auditorium chairs, and a line of coat hooks nailed to a shelf that ran the length of the room. He felt along the shelf. Nothing.

Where else? The laundry basket. He grimaced and shoved one arm into the dirty sheets and clothing, feeling around until he found the faux-silk robe he had worn for his last performance. And there it was. He plucked the wallet out, thumbed through it, and found his identification intact along with one measly Sir Wilfrid Laurier. He shrugged. Que sera sera.

He started toward the window, then turned back, thinking, why not go out the front door?

He was halfway there when he heard a key in the lock. He ducked into the storage room behind the reception area and peered through the louvered divider.

The boss and a man with the face of an eagle entered. The boss went to the desk and switched on the banker's lamp. Silhouettes danced on the opposite wall. Gerald heard the implosion of a butane lighter and smelled cigar smoke. He shifted, feeling a bit silly. Why not just go out and explain to the boss?

Explain what? That he had snuck in through a window he had carelessly left unlocked, jeopardizing his boss's films and God knows what else? He shrank lower. Perhaps he could say he was passing by and noticed the window was open. Felt it was his duty to check things out. Sure, Gerald, he'd believe that. He rocked forward. Maybe it would be best just to tiptoe down the hall and slip out the window.

A fragment of conversation stopped him in his tracks: "I've got six trucks carrying now…" There was a bark of laughter. "…some of it legit." The boss's voice.

The other voice, like nails on a blackboard: "…picking up the shipment on the fifteenth. You come around to the warehouse like always." There was a pause. "You got…?"

"Third door on your right."

Gerald held his breath. He guessed The Eagle wanted to use the washroom. Footsteps passed him down the hall. He heard the boss shuffling through the desk drawer. He hunched lower, squeezing his knees into his chest.

The toilet flushed. The bathroom door opened. Gerald made a face. The pig hadn't washed his hands.

The footsteps returned.

The door beside him flew open. The Eagle stared down at him. Gerald's surprise didn't melt the steel in his eyes.

"What the hell?"

The desk drawer slammed shut. Gerald stood and approached the man, grinning.

"Who — ?" the man began, but Gerald pushed past him and bolted, a few feet ahead of his boss, who bellowed his name as he raced down the hall. He didn't hesitate. He charged into the dressing room, scrambled through the window, and sprinted down the alley.

The headlights of a black Mercedes parked in front of the building flashed on as he clattered onto the sidewalk. The Eagle was at the door, gesturing toward him. He looked frantically for a bus as the car churned into reverse. Then, at the light, he saw a police car. He dashed to the intersection and crossed in front of the cruiser, hovering uncertainly on the sidewalk as the light changed and the police car sped away. But then he saw the police car pull into the Tim Hortons in a mini-mall one block down. He hurried in behind the officers, walked directly through toward the washroom, then ducked out the back door and crept along a row of dumpsters.

He had torn his jacket. "There's four hundred dollars down the drain," he muttered. He peeked around the last dumpster. The fire lane was empty. The last establishment in the mall was a dentist's office. I wouldn't trust my teeth to anyone who practised in this part of town, he thought as he eased along the wall and looked out onto the street. No sign of the Mercedes. The cruiser was still in front of the Tim's. As he watched, the officers came out and got into the cruiser. And then, bumping around the corner and sliding to a stop in front of the mini-mall, a bus. He plunged across the parking lot, holding up his fare.

Chapter Two

Margaret Rudley, co-proprietor of the Pleasant Inn, stood at the front desk, brow furrowed as she reviewed the reservation book. Her husband, Trevor, emerged from the dining room and stepped over Albert, who lay stretched out in the middle of the lobby.

"You're getting good at that, Rudley," she said when he arrived at the desk and put his coffee down. "You didn't spill a drop."

"That dog's like a piece of furniture." He paused as she turned a page. "How does it look, Margaret?"

"A bit nip and tuck. It's as if we were in high season. I have two rooms open in the main house. I have the Oaks available for a week, then Mr. Gregory Frasor checks in. I'll have the High Birches once the honeymooners move out. The Davids will be checking out of the Sycamore in the morning, then I have Mr. Salvadore Corsi in."

"Salvadore Corsi. Sounds like a revolution looking for an island."

"Don't be provincial, Rudley." Margaret reviewed the reservations, then put the book away. "I'm glad we have a little room to manoeuvre. I hate to turn anyone away."

"Definitely our best fall ever." He paused. "It's been a wonderful year, Margaret."

"Knock on wood."

He gave her a jaunty smile. "Oh, I don't think there's any danger of our luck turning." He hummed a few bars of "Sidewalks of New

York" and did a quick sideways shuffle. "The worst is behind us, Margaret. It'll be smooth sailing from here on in."

Adolph checked his watch. Nine-thirty. The dishes were done. He'd run the carpet sweeper over the living-room rug. He was about to lay out his clothing for the next day when the door burst open and Gerald flew in. He ran to his room and hauled a suitcase from the closet. He threw the suitcase onto his bed, tore open the bureau drawers, and began to toss things in the general direction of the bed.

Adolph stopped in the doorway, disconcerted. "Where are you going?"

Gerald gave him a desperate, over-the-shoulder look. "I'm not sure, except out of here."

Adolph moved into the room and sat on the edge of the blanket box. "I thought you were going out to look for your wallet."

"I did."

"Did you find it?"

"Yes." Gerald grabbed a stack of shirts and shoved them into the bag. "That was the good part."

Adolph waited.

"I ended up in the middle of a drug deal going down. A big drug deal. Six trucks."

"Six trucks of cocaine?"

Gerald tore at his hair with one hand and tried to flatten the shirts with the other. "I don't think there are six trucks of cocaine in the country, Adolph. Maybe some. Maybe pot. Maybe counterfeit smokes. A lot."

Adolph pushed his glasses up his nose. "Have you called the police?"

Gerald raised his arms and looked toward heaven. "Have I called the police?" He dropped his arms and began to pace. "I don't think these people would appreciate me going to the police, Adolph."

Adolph half stood, then sat down again. "I don't think you have a choice."

Gerald stopped in front of the window and peered out between the slits in the Venetian blinds. "Yes, I do have a choice. It's between going on the lam or having my arms removed with a hacksaw." He put a hand to his mouth and mumbled through his fingers. "Besides, there's the film."

"The film?"

"Yes, you know the film."

Adolph shook his head, confused. "Why is there a problem with the film?"

"I don't think you want to know."

Adolph spread his arms. "I don't know what you're talking about, Gerald."

Gerald gave Adolph an exasperated look. "Remember I told you the film was a comedy about female impersonators?"

Adolph nodded.

"Well, it wasn't. It was a porn film. Several porn films."

Adolph bristled. "Gerald!"

"Don't Gerald me."

Adolph thought for a moment. "That's despicable, but it's not illegal, is it?"

"No." Gerald put his fingers into his mouth, started to nibble at his nails, then stopped and tucked the hand behind his back. "There's more."

Adolph looked at him over his glasses. "More?"

"It turns out the director was using…youthful actors."

Adolph's eyes widened.

"Do you know what that would do to my reputation?" Gerald fretted.

Adolph glowered. "How could you?"

Gerald flailed his arms helplessly. "Look, during the shoots, I didn't realize they were that young. They looked young. But everybody under thirty looks young to me. I thought he'd just rounded up some particularly young-looking actors because…"

"Because he was hoping to appeal to a particularly scuzzy clientele?"

"I could end up in jail."

"Jail?"

"Yes." Gerald fingered the rhinestone necklace he habitually wore. "So I can't go to the police. And I've got to get out of here because they saw me and they're going to come looking for me."

"You told those awful people where you live?"

"No." Gerald looked to Adolph for comfort, but finding only a frosty stare, turned away. "They know I used to live on Ste-Catherine. They'll find out I moved to St-Henri. Then they'll find out I came here."

"How?"

"These people have their ways."

"What do you mean?"

Gerald turned and grabbed Adolph by the shoulders. "What I mean is they'll threaten my previous low-life, but cowardly, landlords."

Adolph looked weary. "Why didn't you just put in a change of address at the post office?"

"Let's not get into my slothful ways now, Adolph." Gerald shuddered. "These people are not nice guys. They wouldn't think twice about waltzing in here and rearranging my face with a baseball bat. If I'm lucky. If I'm not lucky, they'll put a bullet in the back of my head while I'm on my knees thinking you shouldn't have bothered having the carpets cleaned."

Adolph stared at him. "What about me?"

"Oh, I'm sure they wouldn't have any trouble doing the same thing to you." He returned to the closet and stared desolately at a row of trousers.

Adolph blanched. "We've got to go to the police."

Gerald pulled his head out of the closet. "Listen to me, Adolph. We cannot go to the police. The police cannot protect us. These people don't like snitches." He gave Adolph a haunted look. "They'd torture us to death. Slowly."

Adolph cringed. "What am I supposed to do, Gerald?"

Gerald turned back to the closet. He emptied a shelf of shoes on to the floor, sorted through them, then threw several pairs into a bag, including a pair of black wingtips and a pair of red slingbacks. "You'll have to come with me."

"Where?"

"Where," Gerald echoed, ripping through a bank of hangers. He lingered over a silky item. "I'll never be able to do Judy Garland again. My career is shot."

"For God's sake, Gerald, focus."

Gerald sank down onto the bed. "I don't know." His gaze swept the room. "Gregoire."

"Gregoire?"

"He's an old friend. He's a chef at an inn out in the sticks. Maybe I can stay with him. I'll tell him I'm between jobs."

"What about me?"

"What about you?" Gerald thought for a moment, then brightened. "You could go home."

"What if they find me there? What about my mother?"

Gerald cradled his head in his hands. "Let me think this through." He grabbed tufts of his hair and twisted them through his fingers. "You could get a room at the inn." He lifted his head. "Gregoire will put me up and you can get a room."

"What if they track us down there?"

"How could they track us down there?"

"I'd have to register."

"Adolph, you don't have to use your real name."

"What if they want identification?"

"Say you forgot it. Say you left it in another suit."

"What if I have to sign a cheque?"

"Use cash. They won't ask for your identification if you use cash. We're talking about an inn, not the Chinese border guard."

"How much will I need?"

"I don't know, Adolph. Take what you think you'll need. If it isn't enough, you'll have to check out through a window."

"That's terrible."

"It's better than being killed. Or wishing you'd been killed."

"Then what?"

"Then what what?"

"After I climb out the window?"

Gerald stared over Adolph's head at the wall. "I can't think that far ahead right now. I'll call Gregoire. You call and book a room — once you figure out who you're going to be. Then we'll get our stuff together and get the hell out of here."

"Tonight?"

"We'll spend the night at the bus station." Gerald went to his bedside table and took out a battered leather notebook. He headed for the kitchen with Adolph in tow, tucking the book under his chin while he dialed the number. "Could I speak to Gregoire, please?"

Chapter Three

The phone rang. Margaret glanced at the clock. Five minutes to ten. She shrugged and picked up the phone. "Pleasant Inn. Yes? When would you be wanting it? Tomorrow? Oh, I understand. I often do things on impulse myself." She turned the register to face her. "Let's see. Chalet or main inn? Chalet? We have the Oaks. Yes, it's available for a week. Oh."

Margaret ran a finger down the page. "Sorry, the Oaks is only available this week. Someone who especially wanted an unrestricted lake view reserved for next week. But we could start you at the Oaks and move you to the High Birches. It will be free by then and you could have it as long as you want." She smiled. "It's decided then. Oh, I mustn't forget to take your name. Yes, thank you. We look forward to your arrival." She hung up and wrote, Professor David Wyler: Oaks.

Aunt Pearl was supposed to move back to the High Birches as soon as the newlyweds left but she wouldn't mind staying in her room in the main inn a little longer. She was a good sport. Refusing a guest wouldn't have been appropriate. It wasn't the money. It just seemed wrong to turn someone away. She and Rudley had been known to camp out in the office to accommodate a guest during high season. The bunkhouse had a spare room. It was cheerful and homey. But she didn't like to impose a guest on the staff. They were family, but they deserved their privacy.

The family. She would be glad when Tim got back. It wasn't that she minded waiting tables in his stead — she did that when the inn was hectic anyway — but she missed him. The Pleasant wasn't the same without him.

Rudley hammered down the steps and threw himself over the desk, exasperated.

"Any luck, Rudley?"

He glared past her at the wall. "It was not a mouse, Margaret. Mrs. Sawchuck needs to have her glasses checked. It was one of her hair curlers."

"Couldn't her husband see it wasn't a mouse?"

"Walter could and he did, Margaret. Doreen thought he was just trying to reassure her. When I showed her the curler, she insisted the mouse must have scurried under the bed."

"Did you look under the bed?"

"Under the bed, under the bureau, in the closet. If that cat of yours was worth her salt, it would give the guests confidence."

"It's not her calling, Rudley." Margaret gestured toward Albert, who lay sprawled across the rug, tongue lolling, legs bicycling. "No more than keeping watch is for Albert."

He gave the dog a mournful look. "It seemed a good idea at the time. I thought he might develop into the role."

"He's a sweet dog, Rudley. Would you rather have him snapping at the guests?"

"Depends on which of the guests you're referring to."

"I'm sure if someone broke in during the night, he'd sound the alarm."

"Not unless the intruder tripped over him." Rudley looked up as the door opened. "Officer Owens, what in hell are you doing here?"

The young patrolman paused and glanced around. "I have a couple of tickets to the police banquet."

"That's a strange thing to be doing at this time of night. Selling tickets."

"I'm not selling them. I was just going by..." Owens looked to Margaret.

Margaret came to his rescue. "Were you looking for someone to accompany you?"

He blushed. "Yes."

"When is the event?"

"Next month. The twelfth." He paused. "There'll be a band."

She smiled. "Leave it with me, officer."

"Thank you, Mrs. Rudley." He backed away, narrowly missing Albert, who had chosen that moment to roll over.

Rudley shook his head. "I'm surprised you didn't volunteer me, Margaret."

She gave him an annoyed look. "Don't be absurd, Rudley. Officer Owens was hoping Tiffany would be around."

"Don't tell me he's still carrying a torch for Tiffany."

"Very quietly. I'm afraid Tiffany is quite oblivious."

"A man has to learn to speak up for himself." He squared his jaw. "As I did."

Margaret beamed. "You were a veritable tiger, Rudley." She gave him a peck on the cheek.

Gregoire came out of the kitchen, sweeping his chef's cap from his head.

Rudley turned to him. "And what problem are you bringing me?"

Gregoire drew himself up to his full five feet, three inches. "I do not have a problem. I have brought you a solution."

"Refreshing."

Gregoire turned his attention to Margaret. "That call you put through to the kitchen just before was from a friend I have known almost all my life. He wants to know if he can stay a week or longer at the bunkhouse."

"You know the rules," Rudley said. "He can stay as long as he wants as long as he isn't an arsonist or an exhibitionist."

"He isn't an arsonist," Gregoire said and hastened to add, "I think he is a little short on money. He likes to live more than his means. Anyway, as you know, Melba cannot fill in for supper the next few nights because of her harp recital."

Rudley levered himself off the desk. "I just can't picture Melba on the harp. Must be the cigarette."

"Bluegrass is her," said Gregoire. "In any event, the solution is that my friend is an incomparable waiter. He can wait. Melba can do her harp and Margaret can do her painting without abusing herself, carting around huge platters of my exquisite creations."

Rudley considered this for a moment. "I trust he's reasonably congenial."

"He is like Tim on speed, but he has always been popular with his clientele."

"Tell him, if he'd like to wait, we'll pay him the going rate."

"Thank you."

Rudley paused. "Is that all? Nothing to grouse about?"

"No, everything is perfect."

Rudley looked disappointed. "All right."

"I will say goodnight then."

Margaret smiled. "Goodnight, Gregoire."

Rudley shook his head. "He's Laurel without his Hardy, Abbott without his Costello."

"What were you saying, dear?"

"Tim and Gregoire. Gregoire seems flat without him. They play off each other."

Margaret nodded. "He'll be glad to have Tim back — even if they do argue all the time."

"They're an act fit for vaudeville, Margaret."

"I'm glad we can help Gregoire's friend. Perhaps we can keep him until he finds something else. Perhaps Jim will have a position for him."

Rudley scowled. "The pretty boy from up the bay?"

Margaret smiled. "He is rather handsome."

"He seems like a bit of a dunderhead to me."

"Oh, I don't know. He's made quite a success of his bed and breakfast, and now that he's expanding his guest rooms, I'm sure he'll need to take on some help." Margaret sorted through the reservation list. "I know he'd take Gregoire's friend on if we recommended him."

"We haven't even met him yet."

"If he's a friend of Gregoire's, that's good enough for me."

Gregoire dimmed the lights in the kitchen and picked up the telephone.

Gerald had just locked the door when the phone rang. He dropped his suitcases, fumbled the key into the lock, and dashed into the kitchen. But not in time. The caller had hung up. He played back the message.

"Gerald, it's Gregoire. You should take the bus that gets into Middleton at eleven. If you get off at Lowerton, you can get a ride in with our maintenance man. He will be driving a pickup truck. He is tall and skinny and looks like a psychopathic killer but he is harmless. And if you have a pair of black pants and some white shirts and you want to work, bring them. We will see you tomorrow."

"What was that?" Adolph stood in the doorway.

"Some instructions from Gregoire." Gerald ran back to his room, grabbed a pair of black pants from the closet, rolled them up, and tucked them into his bag. "Okay, let's get out of here."

"Did you turn off the light?"

Gerald pushed Adolph out into the hallway. "The electric bill is the least of our worries, Adolph."

He slammed down the stairs, coaxing Adolph after him, and hailed a cab that was loitering at the corner.

"How much money have you got?"

"Two hundred in cash. I'll get more at the ATM."

"So we're okay." Gerald's eyes searched the dark streets.

"For now," Adolph mouthed. He sank down into the seat, exhausted.

Chapter Four

Morning washed the lake with hazy pastels. A line of geese chattered off the water.

Rudley stood on the veranda, watching as the geese disappeared, their honking finally drowned out by the persistent shriek of a blue jay.

Margaret appeared in the doorway. "A penny for your thoughts, Rudley."

"Wonderful morning, Margaret. I can't remember when we've had a more beautiful fall."

"It's unparalleled." She gave him a kiss on the cheek. "I must get to work. Now that Gregoire's friend is coming to give us a hand, I may be able to sneak out and capture one of these mornings with my palette."

She disappeared into the inn. Rudley inhaled deeply, letting his gaze drift up the lake. Norman Phipps-Walker was out in his rowboat, dozing against his pillow, his fishing line drifting on the water. "I don't know why he bothers with a fishing rod," he muttered.

Rudley braced his hands on the railing and looked across the expansive lawn. Sixty acres of heaven, he thought. Best damned inn in the province. Twenty-six years in the business and he'd never regretted a day. He paused. Never regretted most days. Sublime shoreline, a reed bank that was his pride and joy. Superb collection of Anura. He turned to take in the chalets. Everything in perfect order. Not an inch of flaking paint. He watched as a heron high-stepped along the shore. You could have been a great hoofer, Rudley. The toast of Broadway. But you chose a higher calling. You had to be an innkeeper. He cocked his head to capture the weet-weet-weet of a cardinal, then left the veranda and returned to the front desk.

Tiffany, the maid, was sweeping the lobby.

"Good morning, Tiffany."

She took one hand off her broom, stifled a yawn. "Good morning, Mr. Rudley."

"Late night?"

"The chamber music recital went on and on. The audience demanded encore after encore. Christopher was thrilled."

Rudley rolled his eyes. "Yes, there's nothing like an evening of chamber music." To bore the ass off a water buffalo, he added to himself as she shuffled out of earshot.

Trudy, the waitress, ran up the steps, cheeks aglow. "Good morning, Mr. Rudley. Isn't it a beautiful morning?"

"Good morning, Trudy." He sighed and flopped over the desk. What was with all of this goodness and light? He missed Tim, his unflappable nature, his bad jokes, his irreverence, his sarcastic play-by-play on the passing show. Tim had his flaws — and they were many — but he had a buoyancy that brought the whole place up a notch. A certain touch, an ability to size the guests up instantly, anticipate their needs, play each like a fine violin. He thought of Tiffany's new beau, Christopher Watkins, who played the bass viol. Lugubrious instrument, much like the player himself.

He glanced into the dining room. Melba Millotte was taking an order from Walter and Doreen Sawchuck. The Sawchucks had been coming to the inn for thirty-five years. Every morning, it was the same thing. Two poached eggs with a sprinkle of paprika, two slices of wholegrain bread, lightly toasted, with marmalade on the side, a fruit nappy with three stewed prunes, and two carafes of coffee. He admired the way Tim took the order every morning with a straight face. "Melba can't take their order without puckering her butt."

"She's got a skinny behind," said Lloyd.

Rudley spun to see Lloyd, the handyman, standing behind him with a hammer.

"She does exercises," Lloyd added.

Rudley whipped out the maintenance log. "I think that's enough talk about Mrs. Millotte's derrière. What are you doing this morning?"

"Came to tap down a nail in the floorboard in the hall. Tiffany caught her sock on it."

"Noted."

"Then Mrs. P.W. has a sticky door."

"Appropriate."

"The hinges on the shutters at the Sycamore need oiling."

"Yes."

"Then I've got to fix the counterweight on the kitchen window."

"Ah, yes, wonderful old things. Best invention ever for a window."

"Slick as a goose. Then I've got to go to Lowerton to pick up some spices for Gregoire. And he said to look at the bus for his friend."

"I'll let you at it then."

Mrs. Millotte's voice carried from the dining room. "Now let me make sure I got that straight. Two poached eggs with a sprinkle of paprika. Two slices of wholegrain bread toasted light with marmalade on the side. Three stewed prunes. Carafe of coffee. All times two."

Rudley shook his head. "Never knew she had it in her. The woman has a sense of humour after all."

When the last car dealership faded from view, Adolph sat back and relaxed his grip on his valise.

"Feel better?"

"Marginally."

Gerald broke open a bag of chips. "I told you I'd get you out of this."

"Get me out of this?" Adolph lowered his voice as the woman across the aisle of the bus turned to stare. "Gerald, you're the one who got me into this. I gave you a place to stay. For free. Because you were between gigs and broke. I didn't do anything to deserve this. I had a good job."

"You've still got your job."

"When they find out I've lied to them about the family emergency, I won't."

"Why would they check up on you? You don't make a habit of lying to them, do you?"

"No."

"Who would check up on you anyway? You said your boss is on vacation."

"He's on sabbatical." Adolph sighed. "If he wasn't, he would have insisted on driving me to my mother's. He would have sent flowers." He paused. "I'm not like you, Gerald. It bothers me to take advantage of people."

Gerald stared down the aisle. "It's show business, Adolph. If you want to get ahead, you can't get cold feet about beating someone out of a gig."

Adolph looked hurt. "I guess that's the way it is."

"Besides," Gerald went on, "you've always said the reason you like me is because I'm not boring."

"You've never been boring, Gerald, but why did you have to do that film?"

Gerald grimaced. "I needed the cash. I was counting on that gig at the Carlton."

"You could have sold your video and CD collection."

"I need that stuff to perfect my act." He slumped down in his seat. "I could have been big, Adolph. Bigger than Craig Russell."

"You still can."

"Not unless I get a face transplant." He sighed. "I may be reduced to selling my bod."

Adolph groaned. "Not that."

"There's a niche market of men who get turned on by female impersonators."

"I don't want to hear this. Why don't you get a decent job?"

"Decent jobs are boring."

Adolph pressed his forehead against the window, hypnotizing himself with the stream of cars in the opposite lane, jerking back as a kid in a passing car glanced up at the bus. "All I know, Gerald, is I've never put a toe over the line and I'm on the lam because you got mixed up with an artiste who turned out to be a drug dealer, not to mention a purveyor of kiddie porn." He shook his head. "And signing into an inn under an assumed name — my boss's name…"

"Count your blessings your boss is somewhere out in the wilderness."

Adolph digested this. "What if someone calls my mother?"

Gerald shook his head impatiently. "She's your mother. Give her a call from a payphone when you get into the station. Tell her you've met a girl. That you've gone off with her for a very long weekend. Tell her you gave the people at work a story about having a family emergency. Your mother will be so happy it's a girl, she won't care about you playing hooky. She'll be too busy dreaming about grandchildren."

"Until she finds out I've been murdered because my roommate knew too much."

"They might not kill us. They might just work us over — badly." Gerald's gaze darted over the other passengers. "Try to relax. We're going to what I've heard is a nice country inn. They're going to put you in a nice cottage. There's no way in the world they'd think to look for us there."

Adolph's features smoothed, then froze. "That message your friend left on the answering machine."

"I erased it." Gerald sat back, nibbling on a chip. "I'll get off at Lowerton, meet the hick in the pickup. You'll get off at Middleton and take a cab in."

"A cab?"

"It's only three miles."

"Why can't I ride in with you?"

"We can't look as if we're together." Gerald waved the chip bag at Adolph. Adolph shook his head. "And, once we get to the inn, we can't let on we know each other. Just in case somebody starts putting two and two together." He finished the chips. "One thing I know,

I'll never be able to show my face in Montreal again. I'll have to go overseas, or worse, to Calgary or some other conservative hole. You can go back to Montreal and get on with your life."

"What if they keep looking for me?"

"You may have to get a new apartment and an unlisted phone number. Be discreet."

"Discreet?"

"Change your appearance a bit. Lose the moustache." He crushed the chip bag and dropped it to the floor. "As I've said, Adolph, these are not nice people."

Adolph resumed his miserable watch out the window.

Rudley pulled out the reservation book and examined the guest list. The usual crowd for Halloween: Norman and Geraldine Phipps-Walker and Walter and Doreen Sawchuck, to start with. The Sawchucks had arrived from Rochester flushed with excitement over their custom-made costumes — James and Dolly Madison. Then there was James Bole, an amateur anthropologist of independent means, who, like the others, had been coming to the inn for decades. "I suspect he's studying us," Rudley muttered. "He'll probably write a book about us."

Next were the Benson sisters, who had stayed on at the Elm pavilion instead of making their usual October exit for Guadalajara. "One of these days, we'll winter over," Kate had told him.

Better make it soon, he thought. Louise, the youngest, was eighty-four.

Finally, there was Elizabeth Miller and Edward Simpson, who were arriving next week. He was disappointed they had gone abroad for the summer. "What does Asia have that we don't?" he asked as Tiffany passed the desk.

"Mount Fuji, the Great Wall, the Taj Mahal."

Rudley dismissed this with a sniff. "When is Christopher putting on his next recital?"

"Tonight, as a matter of fact. A singular event. He's doing Mozart's 21st Piano Concerto for the Seniors Association. Solo."

"I've never heard Mozart's 21st done solo on the bass viol."

"That's what makes it a singular event."

"Indeed." Rudley waited until Tiffany trotted up the stairs. "Big geek," he said under his breath. "Looks like an ostrich."

Christopher Watkins was the latest of the young men Tiffany had been keeping company with, all of them artistic types — musicians, painters, poets. He hadn't approved of the painter — arrogant brute. The poet had been equally unsuitable — narcissistic twit. In his opinion, none of them would ever make a living from their pursuits — including Christopher, who, Rudley considered, was lucky to also be a certified public accountant.

He leaned across the desk and smiled. The past year had been the best ever. The fall had been uneventful — well, apart from that ninny-hammer who shot up the pumpkin patch last Halloween. Winter had been Christmas-card perfect; spring, with the Easter Parade, light-hearted — he whistled a few bars of the song and did a lateral shuffle — and summer had passed without incident. Well, no serious incidents. There was the occasion when Norman Phipps-Walker decided to take up waterskiing. But there had been no serious injuries and he had been happy to pay for that chap's canoe. Margaret's first season of summer theatre had been a resounding success. They'd managed *Twelfth Night* and *Carousel*. He'd persuaded Margaret to put off Ibsen for another time. "Preferably forever," he'd added. Margaret had had a successful showing of her watercolours.

He sighed. They'd been operating the Pleasant for twenty-six years and the past year had been without parallel. All they needed now was the return of Tim, the young Paul Newman, waiter par excellence, star of summer theatre, sparkling dancer. Almost as good as myself, he thought.

He returned to the reservation list. Mr. and Mrs. John Smith. A couple flouting their wedding vows, he surmised, something he didn't approve of. "At least they shouldn't be so obvious," he murmured.

"About what?"

"Oh." He looked up as Margaret paused beside him. "This couple that signed in as Mr. and Mrs. John Smith."

"Yes?"

"That's how people sign into cheap motels, Margaret."

"There must be some legitimate Mr. and Mrs. John Smiths in the world."

"I certainly hope so. I wouldn't care to have the reputation of the Pleasant sullied."

"Virtue is a state of mind, Rudley."

"Virtue is a state of mind," he muttered as Margaret moved on to straighten the picture over the mantle. What in hell did that mean? He slumped over the desk. Next thing he knew, Margaret would be petitioning him to let Christopher and his bass viol move into the bunkhouse. Skinny wimp. He wasn't sure if he approved of couples living together, without benefit of clergy. He and Margaret hadn't shared a bed until their wedding night. Although, he thought, rubbing his chin and smiling a jaunty smile, I could have been persuaded. He slammed the ledger shut. He wasn't sure if Christopher was the right sort for Tiffany. She needed someone to keep her grounded. "As Margaret did," he said out loud, nodding confidently.

"As Margaret did what?" she demanded.

"As Margaret did wonderful watercolours."

She shot him a suspicious look.

Rudley returned to his work, humming. Wonderful woman, Margaret. Kind to a fault. Optimistic — even though her optimism was usually quite unwarranted.

He was still humming when the door opened and a chubby middle-aged man entered.

"Mr. Harvey."

"R-R-Rudley." Paul Harvey paused, casting an eye toward the dining room. "I thought I'd stop by and see what you were serving for lunch."

Rudley recited the menu. "Getting tired of your own cooking?"

"If you call fried Spam cooking."

"I understand."

"And the chance for a little intelligent conversation is always welcome. I get a little tired of talking to myself."

"Go ahead into the dining room, Mr. Harvey. In the unlikely event that anyone capable of intelligent conversation shows up, I'll send them your way."

"You've got a great sense of humour, Rudley." Harvey gave him a wave and went on into the dining room.

"I wasn't trying to be humorous," Rudley mumbled. He supposed a man could get hungry for a decent meal and some company, living alone as Paul Harvey did. From what he'd heard, Harvey didn't have much of a social life. He belonged to a couple of clubs but most of the clubs in the village met only every two weeks and not at all during the summer months. He imagined the man got lonely. He knew he would have. He paused, brow furrowing. He'd never lived alone a day in his life. He had gone from a comfortable home in Galt to a university dormitory, then to the hotel rooms he occupied during his hospitality apprenticeship. He wasn't sure if he'd ever eaten Spam. He smiled. He was a blessed man. God knows, man is a social animal, he mused, although he would have gladly eaten Spam from time to time if it meant escaping these ninnies for a few hours.

He opened the accounts ledger and jotted a note. A crash made his hand skitter across the page. He looked up to see Aunt Pearl clutching the newel post. "Pearl, what the hell?"

She dragged herself up. "No harm done, Rudley. I missed the bottom step. Damned trifocals."

"It wouldn't be the Jack Daniels."

She gave him a reproachful smile. "Rudley, you know I don't have a palate for southern spirits." She grabbed his arm for support. "Anything interesting happening this morning?"

"Actually, it's been rather soporific, what with late nights taken up by chamber music and harp recitals."

"I'll be glad when Tim gets back. This place is a grave without him." She gazed dreamily across the lobby. "He's in Acapulco as we speak. That lithe young body sprawled on a white beach under azure skies. The sun, hot, hot, hot. He'll come back bronzed like a god, hair like corn silk. Those blue eyes."

Rudley cleared his throat. "Contain yourself, Pearl. The man's fifty years younger than you."

"I could get around that."

"I don't think you're his type."

She paused. "You're right. I probably can't get around that. What's a girl to do? You haven't booked a single available man in my age group, Rudley."

"I must admit that's a flaw in my booking schedule. I have never inquired in advance about a guest's suitability for my wife's aunt." Who drinks like a fish and steals anything that isn't tied down.

Pearl peered into the dining room. "Is that that nice Mr. Harvey?"

"Yes, it is."

"I've been meaning to get to know him better."

Rudley nodded. "But then you were distracted by Mr. Crowe, then Mr. D'Amato, then Mr. Peabody."

She smirked. "What can I say, Rudley? They swept me off my feet. That Mr. D'Amato. What an operator."

"Mr. Harvey is rather bashful."

"Margaret says he's a gentleman."

"He is that."

"A retired gentleman."

"So I understand," Rudley said absently.

"What did he do?"

"I believe he was a school teacher."

"Do you think he'd be interested in a little company?"

"Don't get your hopes up, Pearl. The man's a virtual recluse."

"Imagine, a dreamboat like that."

"The man is bald and on the heavy side. I know your vision isn't what it used to be, but you're pushing the boundaries of imagination." He took her elbow. "But if you'd like to have brunch with him, I think that could be arranged." He steered her into the dining room. "Mr. Harvey, I believe you've met our Aunt Pearl."

Mr. Harvey stumbled up, making a grab for the chair as it tipped. "Miss Dutton." He hesitated. "Would you care to join me?"

"Don't mind if I do."

"Well, good." Rudley pushed Pearl's chair in. "I'll run around to the kitchen and get you a nice omelet."

"And a half-glass of orange juice."

"And a half-glass of orange juice." Rudley scurried off to the kitchen, reminding himself that he did at least promise Mr. Harvey an interesting tablemate. He barged into the kitchen where Gregoire was putting the finishing touches on a plate of bacon and home fries. He snagged a piece of bacon. "I've dragged Pearl in. Could you make her an omelet?"

"Of course."

"And a half-glass of orange juice."

"To save her the trouble of drinking half a glass before she can empty her vodka into it?"

"Right." Rudley grabbed a cup of coffee and a croissant and returned to the desk. He considered himself a lucky man, with a lovely wife, a beautiful inn, and congenial staff. He reconsidered: Make that a lovely wife and a beautiful inn. He'd even devised a way to keep Aunt Pearl under reasonable control. Amazing what a dash of water in the whisky will do. A duplicitous act, he realized, but what the hell — it saved wear and tear on Pearl's liver. She'll probably outlive us all, he thought, turning to the cupboard door and flinging it open. The handle came off in his hand. "Well," he muttered, "Lloyd will be back soon."

Lloyd could fix anything, and he was good in the garden, too. Rudley often thought the man was capable of being an ax-murderer. He had no evidence to support this belief, but the idea played on his mind from time to time. This morning, though, he waved the thought away and moved his mind toward something more pleasant.

Halloween. He grinned a lopsided grin. That was it! Halloween at the Pleasant was the high point of the fall season. Tim and Margaret would go overboard with the decorations. They'd do the usual spectacles with dry ice and cobwebs fashioned from string and shredded cotton. Margaret could spin webs with the best of them. They'd do the cold hands from the shadows, accompanied by shrieks and maniacal laughter. Doors that opened on squeaking hinges. Tombstones scattered about the lawn. Caskets, some of them yawning open to reveal skeletal remains clawing at the edges. And of course there'd be the apple bob. Pin the tail on the donkey. The pumpkin-carving contest. Mulled cider. All of it capped off with the costume ball. He smiled, did a little shuffle, then fox-trotted across the lobby, neatly sidestepping Albert. "Best hoofer west of the Thames," he said. He turned and ran smack dab into a wisp of a man, holding a valise.

"I beg your pardon," he said. He caught the stranger's nervous look as Albert raised his head. "Don't worry, he doesn't attack except on cue."

"Professor Wyler."

Rudley stared at the man, baffled. Then it came to him. "Oh, of course." He trotted back to the desk and pulled out the register. "Yes, the Oaks." He turned the register toward the guest. "Sign here, please."

The guest hesitated, then took the pen. He scrawled his name, then, looking over his glasses, said, "I don't have any identification."

Rudley gave him a blank look.

"I bought a new wallet. I forgot to transfer my identification."

"Do you plan to do a lot of driving?"

"No. I have cash and traveller's cheques."

"Then you should be all right. As long as you know who you are."

Adolph leaned in and whispered. "Will anyone know I'm here?"

"Do you want anyone to know you're here?"

"No. I'm on sabbatical. You know how hard it is to get time away. When people know who you are and keep wanting things."

"I can relate to that." Rudley went into the cupboard for the key.

"Everyone wants to ask questions."

"What's your field?"

"Uh…English literature. The Romantic poets."

"Well, people would certainly be snapping at your heels if they knew that." Rudley stopped Tiffany who was crossing the lobby. "Tiffany would you show Professor Wyler to the Oaks?"

"Of course, Mr. Rudley."

"The usual orientation."

"Yes, Mr. Rudley."

Tiffany took Adolph's valise and led him off toward the Oaks. Rudley checked the register. Terrible penmanship. He put the register down. "'Oh, to be in England, now that April's here.'"

Margaret paused at the desk. "Rudley, how romantic."

"Our Professor Wyler just checked in. He specializes in the Romantic poets."

"I must see if he'll do some Wordsworth for Halloween."

"Better not, Margaret. He indicated he wants his privacy. Heaven knows the rush that would occur if he started quoting Shelley."

"I do so love Wordsworth."

He folded his hands, looked skyward. "'I wandered lonely as a cloud that floats on high o'er vales and hills.'"

She beamed. "Rudley, you're smashing." She hurried away, humming.

Rudley did a quick patter. "Not bad for a boy from Galt."

Chapter Five

The stairs creaked as Serge and Mitch made their way to the third floor.

Serge paused on the landing. "You could stand to lose a few pounds."

"If you hadn't lost him outside of Tim's, we wouldn't need to be doing this."

"Just shut up and get ready to do the lock." Serge eased down the hallway and stopped in front of Adolph's apartment. "Pretty quiet. The tenants here must actually work for a living."

Mitch bent over the lock. "I got it," he said finally.

"Okay." Serge eased the gun from his belt.

They entered the apartment. Serge jerked his head toward the living room. "Check that out."

Mitch inched his way toward the living room, circled through the kitchen, and reappeared at the door. "Nothing."

"Okay."

They moved down the hall. Serge opened the door to the linen closet and stared at the neat stacks of sheets and towels. "Check the bathroom," he mouthed. He waited in the hallway, gun poised.

"Nothing in here."

Serge stepped around him and flicked the shower curtain aside. They went back up the hallway.

"Nobody home," Mitch said.

Serge went into Gerald's room and kicked aside a pair of thongs. "Looks like somebody left in a hurry." He turned to Mitch. "Go back and put the chain on the door." He poked through the closet, then went into the bedside table and took out some envelopes. There was a credit-card application for Gerald Murphy, half-filled out, and a couple of pieces of junk mail. He grinned. "Look at this," he said to Mitch, who had returned to the bedroom. "Birthday card. Hugs and kisses, Hector." Serge moved to the bureau, opened one of the drawers, and rummaged through. He pulled out a pair of black pantyhose. He threw the pantyhose aside, jiggled open the bottom drawer. "Look," he said, "falsies. They say he does porn. Maybe he's a female impersonator too."

"Maybe he turns tricks on the side."

"Whatever." Serge stood up. "Let's see what's in the other room."

They went into Adolph's.

"Looks like they both left in a hurry, " said Serge. He went to the closet and pointed at a shirt with a button-down collar. "This one looks more conventional." His gaze swept the room. He picked up a picture from the bureau. "Mom and Dad. And their three sons. Heartwarming. Which one do you think he is?"

"Maybe none of them. Maybe he took the picture."

"Maybe he didn't. Take a guess."

Mitch shrugged. "How in hell should I know?"

Serge gave him a disdainful look. "I'd say, by the size of the shirts, he's the shrimp on the end. The one who's about the same height as the old lady."

"So what? We're after the homo."

Serge turned to Mitch and spoke with exaggerated deliberation. "Because the homo probably spilled his guts to the shrimp. Maybe he's his boyfriend. So we got to look for both of them. Maybe we'll get a bonus."

"You think so?"

"No. But if we leave any loose ends, we might get a couple of broken arms." He paused. "Bring that picture." He knelt and shuffled through the bedside table. "This one's a lot neater. Oh, look here, income tax return. Adolph Green. Works at Concordia University. Who in hell would call their kid Adolph?"

"Mrs. Hitler." Mitch sat down on the bed. "So what do we do now?"

"Come with me." Serge led Mitch to the bathroom, looked around, then opened the medicine chest. "See what I see?"

"What?"

"No shaving gear. No deodorant. No combs. I'd say they packed up and left."

"So we've got to put the squeeze on another super."

Serge shook his head. "In case you haven't noticed, this place isn't a roach motel like the others." He wandered out into the hall and checked out the living room before moving into the kitchen. He stopped and stared at the telephone.

Mitch hitched up his pants. "I already checked that. There weren't no messages."

"Look at this, turnip." Serge punched in *69. He listened, then hit a button.

"Good morning. Pleasant Inn."

"Oh, sorry. Wrong number."

"Quite all right."

Serge dropped the receiver into the cradle. "The last person to call here was somebody from the Pleasant Inn."

"So?"

"The guys are missing. The last call they got was from an inn. What do you suppose that means?"

"Nothing. I get stupid calls like that all the time."

"I think it means they hightailed it out of Dodge and maybe got a room at that place." Serge took out his cellphone, punched in a number, and spoke quickly. "Yeah, just to let you know, we got a lead. We had to twist a couple of arms. Nothing serious. They know not to talk. Anyway, we think they're headed for a place called the Pleasant Inn and…"

The voice on the other end cut him off.

"No kidding," Serge said when the voice had finished. "Okay, we'll come by."

He snapped the phone shut and turned to Mitch. "The boss says he knows the place. He's got friends in the area."

Chapter Six

Margaret was putting out flowers in the lobby when Jim Devlin swept in.

"Margaret." He put an arm around her and gave her a peck on the cheek. "Do you have time for coffee?" He glanced up and noticed Rudley glowering at him over the front desk. "Rudley, how are you?"

"Perfect, thank you."

Jim returned his attention to Margaret. "I wanted to talk to you about my watercolours. I'm trying to decide which pieces to take to Portland."

Margaret squeezed his arm. "Here you are, showing your pieces, and all the time telling me you were just dabbling."

His eyes twinkled. "I lied."

I lied, Rudley mouthed.

Margaret took Jim by the arm. "Let's have a spot of lunch. Gregoire's made some wonderful chicken Kiev."

Aunt Pearl wandered in from the drawing room. "Was that Jim?"

"It was."

"Now there's a real Adonis."

"I find him rather ordinary myself."

She smirked. "If that's ordinary, you shouldn't get out of bed in the morning, Rudley."

"I think it's damned silly, a mature woman simpering over a callow youth."

"He's a thirty-year-old hunk."

He folded his arms across his chest. "I won't distinguish that with a remark."

Pearl glanced back into the drawing room where a group of men were gathering around a card table. "I'd better get back to the game. I have a feeling I'm going to have a big afternoon."

"Don't cheat."

"Rudley, what do you take me for?"

"A geriatric alcoholic kleptomaniac. And a nymphomaniac to boot," he said when she was out of earshot. "Adonis," he muttered. "Thirty-year-old hunk."

He reached into a drawer, took out a pack of Benson & Hedges, and lit one. He took a hurried puff. So what if he looks as if he'd stepped off the cover of a Harlequin Romance, he thought. Doesn't have a thing Rock Hudson didn't. Rudley exhaled smoke through his nose. Yes, Jim Devlin was charming. And he supposed he could act. He'd done a passable Billy in Margaret's production of *Carousel*. His singing voice was only a rich baritone, though. Give me a good tenor anytime, Rudley thought. Baritones are pretentious. He supposed, though, he should admire the young man for turning that abysmal brick up the bay into a bed and breakfast. He imagined the renovations had cost a pretty penny. He expected his parents had bankrolled him. "He lacks sincerity," he said out loud.

"Who, Mr. Rudley?"

He looked up to see Tiffany. "Our elected representatives."

Tiffany craned her neck to see into the dining room. "I thought I saw Mr. Devlin come up the walk."

"You did."

"Isn't he charming?"

"If you say so."

He shooed Tiffany away. Of course an impressionable young woman like Tiffany would find this Lothario charming. Look what she had to compare him to — Christopher, that washed out string bean. Of course, Christopher played the bass viol. Rudley scowled. He supposed Devlin was a virtuoso on several instruments. "I can play the accordion," he told Albert.

He suddenly sensed someone behind him. "How in hell did you get in here?" he barked at Lloyd, who grinned.

"I came out of the ballroom and took a left-hand turn in behind you because you said your drawers were sticking."

"They probably just need some Slide and Glide."

"They're all warped and splintered seeing how they get mashed around so much."

"Hmm." Rudley glanced toward the dining room. "What do you think of Devlin?"

"He's kind of friendly and he smells like Gregoire's apple pie. And Aunt Pearl and Tiffany say he looks like a movie star. Tim looks like Paul Newman and Mr. Devlin looks like Pierce Brosnan. And Mrs. Rudley said you look like a movie star too."

"Did she say which one?"

"Don't know. Before I could hear they sent me to get the mail."

Rudley pretended to busy himself with the register. "And what do you think of Christopher Watkins?"

Lloyd grinned. "He's kind of jumpy."

Rudley paused. "Do you think Tiffany likes him?"

Lloyd removed the drawers and stacked them on the desk to show Rudley the damage he'd done. "She likes that he plays the fiddle."

"Do you think she likes him well enough to go away with him?"

"Guess so. She said she's going up to the city with him for the plays."

Rudley started to say that's not what he meant, then changed his mind. "Why don't you take those things down to the workshop and see what you can do with them ." He waited until Lloyd left, then pulled a bottle of whisky from under the desk and poured two fingers into his water tumbler.

He hated the thought of losing any member of his staff. Not that he would tell them that. Take Tiffany. Just a girl, really. Had a master's degree in English Literature — that and a dollar could buy you a newspaper. Tiffany had been at the inn since coming to look for a summer job four years earlier. She seemed content with her situation, he thought. She'd decorated her quarters in the bunkhouse quite tastefully, had taken up writing, and regularly submitted stories to literary magazines. She'd even had some of them published. They were quite good, he considered, although a little arty. She'd always had a reasonable social life, but Christopher had lasted longer than her previous escorts.

He frowned. What if Christopher got a job with a real symphony and left town, taking Tiffany with him? He dismissed the thought. Why would a young girl give up all this for a twit like Christopher? Room to herself. On duty twelve hours a day, six days a week. Excellent working conditions. He took a drink and smiled. Splendid boss.

Lloyd returned. "Just came to measure the gliders."

"At least I don't have to worry about losing you."

"I've got a compass."

Rudley hurried Lloyd through his measurements, then downed the remainder of his drink. The door opened and a small, older man with hazy eyes behind rimless glasses walked in. He carried a suitcase and a garment bag. Rudley stole a glance at the reservation list.

"Roy Lawson," the man said. He nodded toward Albert. "Nice dog."

"He's a treasure." Rudley turned the register toward Lawson. "Room 203. I take it you've come for the Halloween party."

Lawson wrote his name in a fine script. "I didn't know about the party. I'm here on business."

"Oh?"

"Yes, I'm thinking of relocating my optometry practice. I thought I'd look into a few spots in the area." He lowered his voice. "I was thinking about checking into the hotel in Middleton, then I heard how good the food was here."

Rudley drew himself up to his full height. "I can assure you, you won't be disappointed." He took down the key to room 203 and handed it to Lawson. Looking around and seeing neither Lloyd nor Tiffany, he added. "I'll help you with your bags."

"Oh, no need, young man. I think I can manage."

"All right. Lunch is being served now. There's a brochure in your room with the dinner hours. There's a singalong in the ballroom and a euchre tournament in the drawing room tonight."

Roy smiled. "I thought I saw a card game going on in your side room when I came in."

"That would be poker."

"Playing for matchsticks or something more interesting?"

"I would say something more interesting."

"I'll stash my bags and see if I can sit in." He saluted Rudley and trotted up the stairs.

Rudley shook his head. Mr. Lawson was on a fool's errand. He doubted if there was sufficient population in cottage country to support an optometrist. Why was a man of Lawson's age looking for business opportunities anyway? He guessed he didn't have enough sense to retire. A man would have to have an arid mind, he thought, not to have the imagination to enjoy his retirement.

He paused and tugged at his ear. He'd never thought of retiring, really. How could one retire from the Pleasant? He considered this, then brightened. Being an innkeeper isn't a job, Rudley, he said to himself, it's a vocation. One couldn't retire from a vocation. He had responsibilities to his guests, to his staff. The Pleasant was an institution. He was the keeper of a hallowed tradition.

He remembered someone coming around with a survey once. Some damn MBA student. Wanted to know how he ran his inn. How did he spend his days? He hadn't agreed to the project, but Margaret, for some fool reason, had given the young man permission. She had agreed to let him follow her husband around with a clipboard all day, watching him over his glasses and jotting notes. He had later sent along a copy of his results: Time spent at desk, starring into space — forty per cent. Rudley glowered in remembrance. Didn't the young boob know that a great deal of an innkeeper's life involved contemplation, planning? Time spent interacting with staff and guests — thirty per cent. At least, Margaret had commented, he didn't break the interactions down to civilized versus uncivilized. Time spent searching for pieces of paper — twenty per cent. And God knows what he did with the remaining ten per cent, the student concluded. Cheeky, Rudley recalled. I should have complained to his supervisor. Since the young man disappeared the minute the clock struck four, he couldn't have seen what went on all evening. Entertaining the guests, for instance. Discerning. Counselling. Walking the dog.

Albert yawned, dribbling saliva over the rug.

An innkeeper's life is an onerous one, Rudley reflected.

The phone rang. Professor Wyler calling from the Oaks to put in his lunch order.

"May I recommend the spicy gazpacho. The crab cakes are nice today with potato puffs and a crisp chef's salad. There's also a vegetarian pizza with sun-dried tomatoes and feta cheese. Chicken Kiev. Crêpe or omelet of your choice. A sandwich? Of course." He grabbed his pen and scribbled a note. "I'll send it over right away."

He got off the phone and ran into the kitchen "Gregoire, the professor wants a cheese sandwich."

Gregoire rolled his eyes. "I suppose he would like it on gummy white bread."

"Actually, he'd like it on rye. And add a small bowl of clam chowder and a slice of lemon pie. I'm sure he'll eat it if it's on the tray."

"Very well." Gregoire sighed. "One cheese sandwich. Swiss cheese on rye with lettuce." He added a dollop of Dijon mustard and a swirl of alfalfa sprouts and placed a sliced dill at the side. He stood back. "There, there's only so much you can do with a cheese sandwich."

"And you've done quite enough." Rudley grabbed a tray and reached for the sandwich.

Gregoire ladled out the soup, added a sprig of parsley and a sprinkle of fresh-ground pepper.

"Pie." Rudley held the tray out. "And a glass of milk."

Gregoire added a generous slice and a glass of milk.

At that moment, Gerald came into the kitchen, fishing a package of Player's Light from his pocket.

"Going on break?" Rudley asked, regarding his newest staff member, who had arrived the day before.

"Yes."

"Drop this off at the Oaks and take an extra five."

"You've got it." Gerald took the tray and whisked out the back door.

"Energetic," Rudley remarked.

Gregoire checked his gazpacho. "He's as high as a kite almost all the time. Which is a good thing in a wait person."

"Hell to live with."

Gregoire slid a tray of potato puffs into the oven. "Believe me, in the short times I have lived with him, he is murder."

Gerald trotted over to the Oaks, shifted the tray to his left hand, and tapped on the door. The door opened a crack.

"It's me."

Adolph sighed and opened the door.

"Your lunch." Gerald's eyes darted over the cabin. "Why have you got all the curtains drawn?"

"It seems the prudent thing to do."

Gerald set the tray down. "Cheese sandwich? You could eat high on the hog here." He parked himself on the bed and lit a cigarette.

"Are you supposed to be doing that?"

"I'm on break."

"What's going on out there?"

"The usual. People who've been coming here since the Ice Age. They eat a lot, play games, walk around, looking at the flora and fauna. They're having a singalong tonight. I hear the staff takes part."

"Are you going to do your Barbra Streisand?"

"I think I'll just go with the flow."

"They seem like nice people."

Gerald took a long drag and relaxed. "They're dears to work for. The old man yells a lot but nobody pays any attention to him."

"Maybe you could stay here forever."

Gerald rolled his eyes. "I'd be bored out of my skull."

"I wouldn't mind being bored out of my skull, Gerald."

Gerald inhaled briskly. "I must admit there are a few goodies around here. A couple of hunks in for dinner last night. And this older guy, the silver-fox type, I'm sure he's been sending me signals."

"How can you think of that at a time like this?"

Gerald spread his arms. "At a time like what? There is no time here, Adolph. We're timeless. We're in a little bubble, perfectly insulated from the big, bad world. Nothing could possibly happen to us."

Adolph picked up his sandwich, then put it down. "You can stay as long as you want to. I can't."

Gerald jumped up and grabbed an ashtray from the desk. "I couldn't stay here forever, even if I could. I'd go insane. I need bright lights, a little grit and glitz." He paused. "I've been thinking. We can wait this out. Maybe once the big shipment is distributed, once the goods hit the streets without repercussions, they'll figure we didn't squeal and forget about us."

"Do you really think so?"

Gerald sank down onto the bed again. "Nice digs you've got here." He crushed the cigarette and lit another. "No, I don't really think so. They'll harass us to our graves. I imagine I'll have to relocate to Antarctica. But as long as we stay here, we're safe." He gestured toward the tray. "Eat your sandwich. Next time, ask for the crab cakes. They're to die for."

"You're not making me feel any better."

"Look, you're in a nice place. Try to enjoy yourself. Go down to the dining room. Join in some of the activities."

"I'd rather just stay here."

Gerald jumped up from the bed. "Okay, have it your way. I have to get back." He paused at the door. "Is there anything I can get you?"

Adolph followed him to the door. "I wouldn't mind some decent books. The housekeeper keeps bringing me the collected works of dead white men."

"She means well. What do you want?"

"Patricia Cornwell. Perhaps some Peter Straub. I'd like *Koko* if you could find it. I'd feel better knowing someone else is in a bigger horror show than I am."

Gerald patted him on the shoulder. "Don't worry. Everything will be okay. Trust me."

Chapter Seven

"Hold still, Rudley."

Rudley stood in the middle of his office while Margaret took in the ornate waistcoat.

"This is what I get for maintaining my figure, Margaret."

"You haven't gained an ounce since I met you." Margaret stood back to examine the fit. "There it is. Perfect. Try the wig, Rudley."

He let her fuss with the wig. "Lovely idea, Margaret, Louis XVI and Marie Antoinette. But I'm not sure how I feel about you losing your head."

"It has to be done in the interests of historicity." She reached into the box and took out a papier-mâché head. "Magnificent job, if I do say so myself."

Rudley shuddered. "Put it away, Margaret. It gives me the willies."

"That's the point. It's for Halloween." She beamed. "It's going to be perfect, Rudley. The forecast calls for an overcast, wind-tossed night. Imagine. The branches of the oak trees, gnarled arms writhing in the wind, the moon riding scudding clouds. Bats flitting in and out. Lloyd will make a wonderful scarecrow. I can't wait for the children's reaction when he leaves the garden and advances toward the house."

"I don't know about the children but Sawchuck will piss his pants." Rudley took off the wig. "Why on earth did Pearl decide to come as Harry Truman?"

"She's always wanted to wear a bow tie." Margaret put the head back in the box. "The menu will be wonderful as always. Gregoire is making candied apples and popcorn balls for the children. Dozens of assorted cookies. Chocolate and brown-sugar fudge."

"I assume we can put all that stuff in a bag and throw it at them as they come up the walk."

"Be nice, Rudley." Margaret took a program from her pocket. "The children will be touring the sites. Then Tiffany, Lloyd, and I will supervise a special party for them in the coach house."

"In that case, I'll be needed up here to ride herd on the adults."

"Except you will need to make a brief appearance to declare that the mummy has risen."

"I see."

"And that will conclude the program for the children."

"Then the parents will come to pick them up and take them away."

"Some will collect them early, Rudley, but others will want to stay to enjoy the party. Therefore, we'll take turns amusing them. I expect most of them will be collected by ten."

"Sounds pretty grisly, Margaret."

"It will be splendid. And such fun for the children." She patted his arm. "I'm going to take these things upstairs and do the alterations."

Margaret left, humming. Rudley flopped into the chair behind his desk, swivelled to face the wall, and stared at the map of the lake and environs. Almost fourteen months without the flag at half-staff, he thought. No drownings, no accidental poisonings, no dead bodies cluttering up the woods and cabins.

Tiffany was coming to the party as Lucrezia Borgia. Compared to a Borgia, Harry Truman seemed benign. Well, except for that damned A-bomb thing.

Mrs. Phipps-Walker was coming as John James Audubon. He supposed Norman would accompany her as a dodo. The Sawchucks were coming as James and Dolly Madison. Mr. Bole was coming as the Duke of Wellington. He wished Margaret didn't have to lose her head.

He swivelled his chair back to the desk and plunked his feet down on it. He couldn't imagine being married to anyone but Margaret. She had deserted him for the High Birches just twice in the past year, once for calling the president of the Ladies Auxiliary a picklepuss, the other time for insulting her brother Roger: "You know he's sensitive about his middle-aged spread, Rudley." He looked to heaven. "Beer belly's more like it."

Margaret's family had a fondness for the bottle. Witness Aunt Pearl. Margaret was the only one who seemed immune to the habit. He didn't have any moral issues around drink and didn't mind a nip himself now and then. Still, Roger did have an unseemly paunch.

Although Tim hadn't returned from his Mexican vacation, Gregoire said the two of them were coming as Radisson and Groseilliers — as if anyone could imagine that pair exploring North America. Rudley stood and did a sedate dance step across the room. He and Margaret were polishing their minuet. To be historically accurate, he reminded himself. He danced his way to the stairs, then did a Fred Astaire up to the lobby.

He ran into Aunt Pearl, who had paused at the top of the stairs to powder her nose. She snapped the compact shut and tucked it into her purse.

"You look as if you've stuck your nose in a flour bag."

She retrieved the compact, wiped a clear space in the mirror, took out a Kleenex, and removed the blob of powder from the tip of her nose. "Thank you, Rudley. This blasted mirror is useless."

"What are you up to today?"

She checked her lipstick. Scarlet's Passion. "Afternoon tea with the chaps in the drawing room."

"A little Rumoli?"

"Five-card stud."

"How much did you relieve them of last time?"

"A hundred or so, but who's counting?" She snickered. "If I play my cards right, that charming Mr. Lawson might invite me to dinner."

"He has all the charm of a travelling salesman."

"He's a fine specimen."

"If you like overgrown elves."

"He's my age, he's a member of the opposite sex, and he seems to have good bladder control."

"Pearl, everyone knows optometrists are virtually asexual."

She smiled demurely. "Speak for yourself, Rudley."

Rudley watched her feel her way along the wall. "The woman needs cataract surgery, but at least she seems happy," he said to Gregoire, who was crossing the lobby from the dining room.

"She is a walking advertisement for you-are-never-too-old-for-love."

"If you say so."

Gregoire handed Rudley a list. "I have the menu for the children's party."

"Can't they eat what everybody else does?"

"No peanuts or shellfish. And we have to have animal crackers for the canapés, straws with loops, and sprinkles for the ice cream and cookies."

Rudley curled his lip at the list. "Cheese strings and marsh-mallows. They'll be upchucking all night."

"And that is what makes a successful dinner party for kids."

"The little twerps aren't even paying a cover charge." Rudley handed the list back to Gregoire. "At least I get the satisfaction of going down and scaring the hell out of them."

"That should be the icing on your cake."

"Indeed." Rudley checked his schedule. "We're going to have a busy weekend. Tiffany's going to the big city with Mr. Greenjeans. Tim's not back. Melba has a harp camp."

"I hear she's making amazing progress."

"We have a full slate of dinner guests for Saturday."

Gregoire spread his hands. "I don't anticipate any problems. Trudy is always reliable. Margaret will help if necessary. And Gerald is like he is on amphetamines. He could probably handle the dining room by himself."

Rudley lowered his voice. "Is he taking anything illegal?"

Gregoire shook his head. "Never. Gerald has done many crazy things, but he has never done that. He is just a human generator of energy."

"Refreshing," Rudley murmured as Gregoire left. "Someone who works full tilt and never complains. We could use more of that." He paused as Gerald flicked past the door. "Or perhaps not."

He couldn't fault Gerald as a waiter. He showed up on time, was pleasant, attentive to the guests, and got along well with the rest of the staff. But he realized he didn't want Gerald around forever. All that activity would drive him nuts eventually. He preferred the contemplative life, far removed from the hustle and bustle of city life, like Thoreau at Walden. Rudley shrieked as a drawer opened behind him. "What are you doing here?" He turned to face Lloyd.

"Looking for my jackknife."

"What would your jackknife be doing in my drawer?"

"Put it there." Lloyd pulled out another drawer and sorted through it. "Here it is." He grinned. "Wanted to make sure I knew where it was. For my jack-o'-lantern." He returned the knife to the drawer.

"You can leave now," said Rudley.

"Yes'm."

Rudley pulled out his package of cigarettes. Of course, he thought, Thoreau didn't have to put up with this crowd.

Chapter Eight

The sun had set hours before. The dining room had shut down, the chatter of dishes and clatter of silverware now absent. Rudley lounged against the desk, sipping coffee and reading a creased copy of the *Globe and Mail*.

"Rudley." Geraldine and Norman Phipps-Walker appeared before him.

Rudley lowered his paper. "Mrs. P.W., Norman." He gestured at the device Mrs. Phipps-Walker had strung around her neck. "Doing some night photography?"

"We hope."

"We're looking for the great horned owl tonight," Norman said as if he were announcing he was looking for his shoes.

Mrs. Phipps-Walker removed a box from her pocket. "We're also hoping to get a recording."

"Perhaps we could feature that at Music Hall."

"Wonderful idea," said Norman.

"We're optimistic we'll have a good experience tonight," said Geraldine.

"Lovely evening for it," said Rudley.

"We couldn't have asked for better."

"Planned it myself, Mrs. P.W."

She stared at him for a moment, then smiled. "You're a caution, Rudley." She started toward the door. "Come along, Norman."

Rudley watched them leave. Norman has been trailing after Geraldine for forty years, he mused as he straightened the newspaper and picked up his cup. He paused to stare dreamily across the lobby. The evening was perfect, with the quiet glow of the lobby, the dining room dark and silent, the gentle click of dice from the drawing room, and the occasional burst of laughter from the gentlemen enjoying cigars on the veranda. In an hour or so, he would call it a day and retreat to his quarters with a good suspense novel and a glass of Chivas Regal. He glanced at the empty spot on the lobby carpet. Margaret had taken Albert for a walk along the shore. No need to worry when she's with Albert, he thought. She'd fight to the death to save that slavering behemoth. He took a deep breath and smiled. The life of an innkeeper, he thought, was onerous but damned near perfect.

Gregoire gave the kitchen a final inspection, turned off the overhead lights, tossed his apron into the laundry hamper, and let himself out the back door, locking it behind him.

A glass of wine, a little light opera, and to bed for a well-earned few hours. He sauntered down the path to the bunkhouse.

When he arrived, Gerald was modelling a shirt in front of the hall mirror. "Do you like this?"

Gregoire studied the silk Art Deco print. "Very nice."

"Or what about this?" Gerald ran to his room and returned with a flaming red number. "With black leather pants."

Gregoire went to the kitchen and poured a glass of chardonnay. "It would be a big hit in Amsterdam. Otherwise, it's a bit much. Where are you planning to wear it?"

"I have a date."

"A date?"

"Yes." Gerald checked his image in the mirror and flicked back a lock of hair. "The Silver Fox."

"I beg your pardon?"

"Mr. Salvadore Corsi."

Gregoire paused, his lips kissing the rim of the wine glass. "Mr. Corsi?"

"Yes. Didn't you notice? He's been making eyes at me since he got here."

Gregoire put his glass down. "No, I didn't notice. I am too busy in the kitchen to notice that the waiter is hustling the guests."

Gerald smoothed his lapel. "Don't be a prude."

"I am not being a prude. It is not proper to date the guests."

Gerald waved him off. "You don't have to yell. I have ulterior motives."

"I don't care what motives you have. It is not right."

"The man's a filmmaker. He does documentaries. A guy has to take advantage of his opportunities in this business. Who knows? He might want to do a documentary on female impersonators."

"That is even worse. Not only are you dating a guest, you plan to take advantage of him."

"In all the ways I can."

Gregoire drew himself up to his full height. "I will not let you do this."

Gerald gave him an oblique look. "What are you going to do about it?"

Gregoire picked up the telephone. "I will call him myself. As chef and captain of the dining room. I will tell him it is against the policy of the Pleasant Inn for the staff to meet privately with the guests."

Gerald caught his arm. "Oh, don't be such a goody two-shoes. This is the opportunity of a lifetime. Do you think I'm going to pass it up because it violates some old crab's silly rules?"

Gregoire removed Gerald's hand. "Rudley may be an old crab, but he took you in when nobody else was seeming to want you and gave you a job and a nice place to stay."

Gerald opened the door and stepped out onto the porch. "Good night, Gregoire."

Gregoire ran to the door, shouting after him. "This is the last time. You will not get away with this with me again."

"Poo to you," Gerald called over his shoulder.

"I warn you…" Gregoire stopped, his face flushed. "Good evening, Mr. and Mrs. Phipps-Walker."

Chapter Nine

Rudley woke to a familiar sound. He leapt out of bed and seized the alarm clock. Twenty minutes past five. He looked over at Margaret. She was sleeping soundly.

"Damn sirens," he muttered. "They're so common now, they might as well be loons."

He threw on his bathrobe and ran down the stairs, pausing at the dining room door to catch a whiff of Gregoire's wonderful coffee. There was none.

He charged into the kitchen. The lights were on. Ingredients for omelettes and pancakes, waffles and muffins sat on the counter. A bowl of fruit glistening with water droplets cozied up to the juicer. The coffee urn waited, ready to be turned on.

"Gregoire?"

He checked the pantry, opened the back door, and stepped out onto the porch. The morning mist lay like a blanket two-feet deep across the lawn, shredding at the edges with dawn's first light. It was thick, but not thick enough to obscure the red and blue flashing lights in the lane behind the bunkhouse. He secured his bathrobe and scurried across the lawn, coming to a halt at a line of yellow tape. Beyond the tape, two police cars and an ambulance squatted in the shadows. A uniformed officer and a civilian in a blue windbreaker and grey chinos huddled together at the shore. A little man in khakis and a straw hat stood outside the tape.

Rudley stopped short of the tape. "What in hell is going on?"

The uniformed officer turned. "Mr. Rudley. How kind of you to grace us with your spindly white legs at this hour in the morning."

"Ruskay." Rudley glared at the officer, then turned to the man in the straw hat. "Norman what are you doing out here?"

Norman gave him a blank look. "Trying my luck as usual."

"In a fog bank like this?"

"I thought it might be clearer out in the middle."

Ruskay returned his attention to the lakeshore.

"What in hell is going on here?" Rudley repeated.

"Well," said Norman, "I got fifty yards out or so and still couldn't see my hand in front of my face, so I decided to return to the shore. Except I couldn't see the dock. I didn't want to run the boat aground so I decided to make a soft landing in the reed bank. I searched until I found the spot where the reeds thin. I had almost reached shore when I ran into him." He shook his head. "I couldn't believe what I saw."

Rudley gave him a pleading look. "What did you see, Norman?"

Norman bowed his head. "I know you don't want to hear this sort of thing, but there was a man hanging over the bank with his head and shoulders in the water. He was practically naked. Gregoire was bending over him. I called to him: 'Gregoire, help me get him out of the water.' He looked up at me. His eyes were like saucers, gleaming white through the fog. Finally, he responded. We hoisted him out of the water. It was then I realized it was Gerald."

"Gerald?"

"Dead as a doornail."

"Dead?"

"We tried, Rudley, but we couldn't do a thing for him. I suppose we shouldn't have taken him out of the water before the police arrived. I suppose we destroyed evidence, but we couldn't tell for sure he was dead. When it was clear he was, I called the police." He produced a cellphone from his pocket. "With all that goes on around here, I decided it was prudent to carry a telephone with me at all times."

"Gerald? Our Gerald?"

"I'm afraid so, Rudley." Norman observed a moment of silence, then said, "The police questioned me, then they questioned Gregoire, then they took him into the back of the cruiser for further interrogation." He gave Rudley an oblique look. "They were friends weren't they? Gerald and Gregoire?"

"Yes."

"This is the first time we've had a body around here near and dear to someone."

Rudley's mouth drooped. Damn, Gerald, Gregoire's old friend from grade school. He understood they hadn't been close in recent years but still... He thought of Squiggy Ross, his childhood playmate, the cute little boy with the blond curls and gap-toothed smile. Damon and Pythias, they had been. He hadn't seen Squiggy in years. He'd turned into a toothless rummy, as bald as a cue ball. Sat around on corners, begging for change. Still, if he heard Squiggy had drowned...

"They had an argument last evening, on the steps of the bunkhouse," Norman went on. "Geraldine and I heard them." He gave Rudley an apologetic shrug. "I didn't mean to implicate Gregoire, but the argument came up in the line of questioning. By the police. Geraldine and I weren't the only ones. The Sawchucks were taking a stroll nearby. They also heard the argument."

"What were they arguing about?"

"I don't know, but Gregoire was clearly upset. He was screaming at Gerald: 'You won't do this to me again,' he said. And Gerald replied: 'Poo to you.'"

Rudley's brow wrinkled. "'Poo to you?'"

"Yes. And then Gregoire said: 'I warn you.' At that point he saw us and went into the bunkhouse."

Rudley glanced toward Ruskay. "You're sure he was dead when you pulled him out of the water?"

"I'm afraid so."

"Well, damn." Rudley waved to get Ruskay's attention. "I want to talk to Gregoire."

Ruskay sauntered over to the tape. "I'm afraid not. We're about to take him to the station."

"What in hell for?"

"We need to question him further."

"How much further?"

"I can't say." He took a roll of police tape from his pocket. "We're going to cordon off the bunkhouse. No one's allowed in."

"Now see here, Ruskay."

"We're waiting on a search warrant." Ruskay turned away.

Norman tugged at Rudley's sleeve. "Who's going to fix breakfast, Rudley?"

"Lloyd" — Margaret put a tray on the trolley — "take this to the Sawchucks, please. And if anyone's waiting, find out what they want."

"Yes'm."

"That's a dear."

Rudley stood over the counter, hacking up strawberries and melon. "After what's happened, those philistines should be satisfied with toast and coffee."

Margaret patted her forehead with the tail of her apron. "We have to carry on, Rudley. Mind you don't bruise the strawberries."

"I don't know why they had to take Gregoire to the station. I don't know why they won't let us talk to him."

"I suppose they don't want us interfering with the investigation."

"Since when have we interfered?" Rudley paused to mop up juice from the mangled strawberries. "Ruskay knows Gregoire wouldn't kill anyone."

Margaret sighed. "Who knows what any of us would do in the heat of passion."

"I hope you're not going to say that when they ask — as they inevitably will." Rudley put the knife aside and pulled out a tray of fruit nappies.

"I'll be discreet."

"If that damned Phipps-Walker had only kept his mouth shut."

"The police would have heard about the argument one way or another."

Rudley grabbed a tray of croissants. "No, they wouldn't have. Not one of them could find his head if it weren't attached to his shoulders."

"Be nice, Rudley."

Lloyd returned with the trolley. "Mr. Bole wants blueberry pancakes and sausage. He says he wants the pancakes with two pats of butter put on just as they come off the griddle, and maple syrup on the side. Warmed."

"Tell Mr. Bole to take a flying leap."

"And the sausage. Three of them, with a dollop of mango chutney on the side. A garnish of thin-sliced orange and strawberries cut in quarters with a sprinkle of cinnamon sugar. He says Gregoire would know how to do it just so, but you would have to be told."

"Mr. Bole is just being helpful," said Margaret as Rudley's face turned red.

"And Mr. Sawchuck said to tell you the coffee was —"

"Tell Mr. Sawchuck —"

" — the best he's ever had."

"Well, we have at least one guest with a discriminating palate."

"Lloyd, dear, would you go into the pantry and bring out another tray of eggs?"

"Yes'm."

"We'll get by, Rudley." Margaret gave his arm a squeeze, leaving a handprint of flour. "Gregoire will be back by lunch. Everything will be all right." She paused. "Poor Gerald. It will be a while before everything is normal again."

He glared at the wall. "It seems to me, Margaret, everything is entirely normal."

A dusty grey sedan pulled up to the bunkhouse. Detectives Michel Brisbois and Chester Creighton got out. Brisbois, the older of the two, started to button his jacket, then gave up. Creighton tall and angular, stretched and yawned. Ruskay trotted down to meet them as they advanced toward the lakeshore.

"I was planning a quiet day reading the *Sunday Star*, Stan," Brisbois said in greeting. "I'd like to hear some compelling evidence that this is a murder scene."

"Well, sir," Ruskay began, "it was the way they found him. His head and shoulders were in the water. The rest of him was sprawled on the bank."

Brisbois took out his notebook. "Had he been drinking?"

"No evidence of that so far."

"Drugs?"

"Nothing on him. Nothing in the bunkhouse except a bottle of Tylenol. There was half a bottle of wine and a six-pack in the refrigerator."

Brisbois' eyes drifted over the body. "Who's the victim?"

"Gerald Murphy. He's been working here as a waiter the last two weeks."

Brisbois made a note. "Who found him?"

"Gregoire. Then Phipps-Walker came by in his boat. He states he found Gregoire kneeling over the victim."

"Phipps-Walker? That old coot's here again?"

"Yes. He says Gregoire's eyes were like saucers. That he had to prompt him to get him to help get the guy out of the water."

"Okay."

"They got him out. Tried to do CPR. No luck. Phipps-Walker called 911 on his cellphone. The call was clocked at headquarters at ten to five."

"Around five. How come Gregoire wasn't in the kitchen?"

"Says he was. Went up at four, as always. Phoned down at a quarter to five to wake Gerald up. Didn't get an answer. Came down to the bunkhouse. Found Gerald's room empty. Went looking for him. Almost tripped over him. Then Phipps-Walker came out of the reeds in his boat."

"What in hell was Phipps-Walker doing in the reeds?"

"He said he was fishing."

Brisbois massaged his forehead. "Go on."

"The deceased wasn't wearing anything except a pair of red jockey shorts. The coroner thought they were silk." He looked to Brisbois for validation of his opinion of this perversion. Brisbois merely shrugged so he went on. "There were clothes strewn around his room. Apparently, he was out last night. Had a date. Nobody seems to know what time he came in."

"Okay."

"There's a bit of a mess in the room. The doily on the night table's half off. There's some stuff on the floor — one of those mini-flashlights, a watch, some change. Otherwise, nothing."

"What about his wallet?"

"In his pants pocket. Looked intact. Identification. A few dollars."

"Door jimmied?"

"No sign of that. According to Gregoire, both the doors — the victim's and the main door — were ajar when he came up."

"Did he lock the main door when he went up to the kitchen?"

"No. Apparently that's usual."

Brisbois shook his head. "Given that they had a murder here last year, you'd think they'd lock up like Fort Knox." He thought for a moment. "So the guy gets up. He's been out late. Goes outside to clear his head. Maybe he dunks his head in the lake, except he goes too far forward, panics and drowns."

Ruskay's shoulders sagged.

Brisbois pushed back his hat. "I'm simply offering an innocent explanation. I agree it doesn't smell right."

"There's another thing."

"Okay."

"Witnesses overheard them — the victim and Gregoire — having an argument last night."

"Time?"

"Around ten. The Phipps-Walkers were out looking for birds. And Walter and Doreen Sawchuck, they were taking a walk along the shore. Gregoire and the victim came out onto the porch. I guess it was pretty loud."

"Could they tell what the argument was about?"

Ruskay consulted his notes and read back what Norman had told him.

"'Poo to you?'"

"Yeah. When Gregoire saw the Phipps-Walkers he broke it off and went back inside."

"What does Gregoire say they were arguing about?"

"He refused to say. That's why we took him in."

"And locked him up?"

Ruskay flushed. "He's a suspect. He refused to cooperate. He was at the scene. They'd had a fight."

"It's okay, Ruskay. You did the right thing." Brisbois turned to Creighton who was conferring with an officer on the bank. "What do you see, Creighton?"

Creighton stuffed his hands into his pockets. "Not much. Rudley keeps things pretty tidy. A stray butt or gum wrapper would stand out like a sore thumb. There's a mess of footprints in the soft soil near the edge. The team lifted a couple, but there were a lot of different people around — Phipps-Walker, Gregoire, the paramedics."

"Was our victim wearing shoes?"

"No."

"Any barefoot prints?"

"No."

Brisbois nodded. "Okay." He motioned to Ruskay. "Back up a bit. What did Gregoire say exactly about his itinerary this morning?"

Ruskay thumbed through his notebook. "He says he got up at a quarter to four. He showered, shaved, dressed. He was in the kitchen at five after four. At a quarter to five, he called the victim to wake him up. Apparently, Gerald wasn't used to the early hours they keep around here. He didn't get an answer so Gregoire went down to the bunkhouse."

"So he got down here around a quarter to five."

"Yeah."

Brisbois paused to follow the flight of a pair of ducks. "Any idea how long the guy's been dead?"

"The coroner thought not long, maybe a couple of hours on the outside."

"Strange." Brisbois took a few steps away, turned back. "Did Gregoire see him before he went up to the kitchen?"

"He says he didn't."

"Did he see him come in last night?"

"No."

"Do we know if he came in last night?"

Ruskay scratched the back of his neck. "Gregoire said the victim left his door open when he went out last night. It was closed when he got up this morning."

"So somewhere between four and five, the victim ended up in the drink. Unless he wasn't in his room. In which case, he could have been in the drink before Gregoire went up to the kitchen. Assuming Gregoire's telling the truth."

Creighton chuckled. "You don't seriously believe Gregoire killed that guy."

Brisbois gave him a sharp look. "I don't know anything at this point. Phipps-Walker could have done him in for all I know." He turned back to Ruskay. "Did Phipps-Walker volunteer this information about the argument out of the clear blue?"

Ruskay thought for a moment. "No. I asked him if the two guys knew each other. He said he understood they both lived in the bunkhouse, then he added that bit about the argument."

Brisbois frowned. "What about the rest of the staff, the ones who live in the bunkhouse?"

Ruskay consulted his notes. "The maid, Tiffany Armstrong, she normally lives there, but she's in Toronto for the weekend. The waiter, Tim McAuley, he's on vacation in Mexico. The maintenance man, Lloyd, he's still camping out in that shed behind the inn. I guess he doesn't move into the bunkhouse until the lake freezes over."

"Yeah, I remember that." Brisbois smiled, recalling a previous murder he had investigated at the Pleasant. "Something about getting more fresh air." He sobered. "So, it was just the two of them in the bunkhouse last night."

"As far as anybody knows."

"Any history of bad blood?"

"Nothing I've heard so far. Rudley says Gregoire asked him to take Gerald on because he was between jobs and short on cash. They expected he'd be around for two or three weeks but they were planning to keep him on until he got something else."

"Didn't rub anybody the wrong way?"

"Nope."

"Anybody have any idea where he went last night?"

Ruskay shook his head.

"Okay." Brisbois reached into his pocket and took out a package of Nicorette gum. He looked at it, put it back, and took out a pack of du Maurier instead. He lit one. "Let's take a look through the bunkhouse," he said to Creighton. "Then we'll go back to Middleton. Look in on Gregoire." He turned to Ruskay. "Get a list of all the guests who've been here since Gerald arrived."

Creighton grinned. "Don't you want to go up to the inn and bug Rudley?"

Brisbois shook his head. "I think we'll put that off as long as possible."

Chapter Ten

"I must say, Rudley," — Mr. Bole looked over his half-glasses at Rudley, who loomed over him, crushing the hem of his apron with his right hand — "these pancakes are a bit dense."

"They're hardy, Mr. Bole. It's my grandmother's recipe."

"Then I suggest you give it back to her." He paused. "Do you have any of those frozen ones kicking around? You just put them in the toaster. Can't go wrong."

Rudley swept up the offending plate. "I'll give it another try." He scurried back to the kitchen. "Margaret, Mr. Bole insulted my pancakes."

"I'll have Lloyd do up a plate for him. The Phipps-Walkers raved about the batch he did for them."

Rudley glared. "If they'd taken a good look at his fingernails, they would have ordered out."

"Be nice, Rudley." Margaret lowered her voice. "Lloyd's an orphan."

Lloyd grinned. He wasn't an orphan, but since this bit of fiction brought extra pieces of pie and endless sympathy from Mrs. Rudley, he was happy to maintain it. "You got to get the grill hot so the little drops of water hiss and scoot," he explained. "Then you got to wait until the whole upside of the pancake is covered with little bubbles. Then turn it over and wait just so."

"I think that's the problem with yours, Rudley," Margaret said. "You aren't waiting."

"I don't have time to wait. I have an inn to run. Have you heard back from Cooper?"

"He's just been taken on at the Water's Edge."

"Farrell?"

"He's gone back to Ireland. He was offered a wonderful job in Dublin."

"Call Cooper and offer him double what Watt's paying him," Rudley said. His words pained him.

"We can't poach other people's chefs, Rudley. You wouldn't want anyone to do that to us." Margaret patted her brow. "I've left a message for Mr. Cadeau. I know he's available." She met Rudley's stare. "They let him go from the Water's Edge."

"What was he trying to do? Palm off a bear as filet mignon?"

"I think the Watts got tired of his temper. He did very well when he filled in for us last time."

"He's a pain in the ass."

"We need him, Rudley. The guests have been patient. We'll ask him for the week. I'm sure Gregoire will be back by then."

"What in hell are they keeping him for?"

"I suppose it's because of the bad luck they had last time, Rudley. They gave their suspects free reign." She lowered her voice. "You know what happened last time."

"I know what happened last time, Margaret."

She eased the spatula from his hand. "Rudley, why don't you go out to the desk? We can manage here."

Lloyd grinned. "Probably better."

Brisbois returned to the interview room with a cup of coffee and closed the door behind him. He spread out his notes and perused them, tapping his pencil against the table.

"Gerald wasn't drunk and we don't have anything so far on the tox screen," he said to Creighton. "He didn't drown. He was smothered. In his own bed. Probably with that pillow we bagged. Pathologist notes bruising on his chest. Pre-mortem. Suggesting someone sat on his chest while they were smothering him." He grimaced. "Nice. He was then dumped upside down in the lake to make double sure." His brows arched. "Look at this. His toes were dirty. Dorsal surface. But the soles were clean."

Creighton looked up from his notes. "Dorsal. That's the top?"

"Yeah."

"He was dragged out face down."

"And what does that suggest?"

Creighton shrugged. "Maybe two people."

Brisbois cocked an index finger at him. "Could be. One person would have dragged him out backwards. Face up. The dirt would have been on his heels. Two people? They probably dragged him out, one under each arm."

Creighton tore a piece from the edge of his Styrofoam cup and flipped it into the ashtray. "It's hard to imagine Gregoire being involved in that."

"The Crown didn't think so." Brisbois shrugged. "It's hard to see him getting a body out of the bunkhouse by himself. But he could have. As for smothering him, it wouldn't have been that hard. The victim's asleep. Completely off his guard. Even if he woke up, what does he see? Gregoire. He wouldn't see any danger. After that? Well, I wouldn't want to have Gregoire sitting on my chest. He's built like a fireplug."

"Gerald was quite a lot bigger. He could have bucked him off."

"Maybe he woke in a state of panic, confusion. He didn't think about what was on his chest. He was pawing at the pillow."

Creighton gave him a look. "I don't know about you, but I can't see Gregoire doing something like that, even if he could."

"Okay." Brisbois reviewed his notes. "Gerald was going somewhere. Where did he go? Who did he go with?"

"That we don't know. Yet."

Brisbois bounced his pencil off the table, caught it. "What I don't get is why Gregoire won't talk to us. Tell us what they were fighting about."

"Either he's guilty or he's protecting someone."

Brisbois tugged at his collar. "What did you get on those phone calls of yours?"

Creighton picked up his notes. "Gerald Murphy. Last worked as a waiter at Le Cirque Rouge in Montreal. He also did a floor show there. Female impersonator. Specialized in Judy Garland and Barbra Streisand." He shook his head. "Don't these guys have any imagination? They're always Judy or Barbra."

Brisbois waved his pencil to urge him on.

"Anyway, he lost his job at Le Cirque when the place closed. Rent got too high. The address they had on him was a non-starter. The landlord said Gerald moved out without leaving a forwarding address. His boss, Guy Lambert, said he was a good waiter and did a good show. He didn't know much about his private life. Said he was very big on making a name for himself in show business."

"We'll have to follow that up."

"Yeah. The police down there have never had any dealings with him. He didn't have a car. Didn't even have a telephone in his name. Apparently, he got cut off almost a year ago for non-payment."

"How did he contact his family?"

"His family hasn't heard from him in months. His brother said that wasn't unusual. They expected to hear from him when they heard from him. He always checked in eventually."

"Except this time."

"Except this time."

"No friends?"

"Like with the family. He didn't exactly live in their pockets. I talked to one of the waiters. She said he was fun to work with, but superficial. Said he was kind of a user."

"Same as with Gregoire," Brisbois said. "Maybe Gregoire didn't like that. Okay" — he pushed back his chair — "give me the rest."

"Gerald Murphy led a pretty normal life," Creighton editorialized, "until he graduated from kindergarten. Born in Newcastle, New Brunswick. Parents were George and Betty. Brothers Michael and Kenneth. Father was a machinist. Mother worked in a nursing home. Father died four years ago. Mother and brothers still live in Newcastle. The brothers are both teachers. Gerald received the standard Catholic-school education. Went to Mount Allison. Left without taking a degree."

"Did they say why?"

"His brother Michael" — Creighton flipped a page — "said he got bored. Moved to Quebec City. Worked at a place called Le Canard Sauvage, a dinner-dance club. Gay male exclusively. The manager, Chris Brown, describes him as swish."

"What did he do?"

"Waited tables. Did an act. Apparently, he was working up a Diana Ross routine. Guess it didn't work out."

"He didn't include it in his Montreal act."

"No." Creighton flipped a page. "He was in Quebec City four years, then took his act on the road. Caribbean. Worked in the resorts. We've put in a request to the police in Bermuda and Barbados. Nothing yet." He studied the page for a moment. "Then he went overseas, Germany, the Netherlands."

"Waiting tables?"

"Yup. He also did some impersonations there."

"You got that from Brown?"

"No, Deiter Bruhner. I got his name from Lambert in Montreal. Deiter worked with Gerald in a club in Amsterdam. He sort of confirms what everybody else says. Flamboyant. A user. He said Gerald also dabbled in the sex trade. Occasionally. If he saw something he wanted and didn't have the cash."

"Did he have something going on with Deiter?"

"Not much. They were mainly friends. Deiter came to Montreal to attend McGill. That's how I found him. Through the alumni review. He looked Gerald up when he was here. They got together from time to time. Seems to be a pretty decent guy. He said Gerald was a lot of fun to be around, but a bit wearing after a while. Always revved up. Always short of cash. Superficial in his relationships."

"Doesn't seem like much of a life, does it?"

"How so?"

"Transient. No ties. Goes to university and ends up waiting tables."

Creighton shrugged. "Hey, he's a single guy. Hopping from one playground to another. Lots of boyfriends. Having a good time. Maybe, once in a while, he thought about finishing his degree, getting a nine-to-five. Drudgery. Responsibility. Then he looked out over those Caribbean waters and said, 'What the heck. Life is good.'"

"So why would he come back?"

"Maybe he got homesick."

"He's in some exotic locale and he gets homesick for Newcastle, New Brunswick?"

Creighton flipped through a few pages. "What did Deiter say about that? Oh, yeah. Gerald met some guy, a porter on the Royal Dutch Lines. He thought that sounded pretty spiffy, so he signed on as a waiter. By the time they got to New York, the whirlwind romance had run its course. The waiter stayed on the boat. Gerald got off and hightailed it home to Newcastle where, according to his brother, he stayed long enough to get fed and have his laundry done. Then he's off, this time to the Laurentians where he got a job at a resort — the Windmills — thanks to Gregoire who was working as a chef there. That's just before Gregoire came to the Pleasant. Anyway, Gerald got bored with the Laurentians in pretty short order. Took off to Montreal. Worked there until Le Cirque closed down. Next thing we know, he shows up at the Pleasant. Gets a job. Once again, thanks to his friend, Gregoire."

"Why wouldn't he just look for another place in Montreal?"

"Sounds as if he was broke. Big cities are expensive. Maybe he couldn't get things together fast enough."

"He's thirty-five years old, no responsibilities, and he's broke?"

"He lived beyond his means." Creighton threw up his hands. "I mean, how many pairs of silk jockeys do you have? This guy had twenty. His socks were a disaster, but he had twenty pair of silk shorts."

"Socks don't go with heels anyway." Brisbois looked at his notes. "So he left Le Cirque four months ago. He hasn't been at that address he gave Le Cirque for six months. Where in hell has he been?"

"We don't know."

"The guy had to leave a trail. At least a utility bill."

"Unless he got a place with utilities included. Or maybe he moved in with somebody our informants don't know about."

Brisbois gave him a disparaging look. "Hey, even we can't be that unlucky."

Chapter Eleven

Rudley leaned over the desk. "Why would a man who wanted to succeed as a female impersonator call himself Gerald?"

"I don't suppose he had a choice, Rudley. His parents probably called him Gerald."

"People change their names all the time. You'd think he could have come up with something more appropriate."

Margaret gave him a bewildered look. "If you were a female impersonator, what would you call yourself?"

Rudley thought for a moment. "Well, I don't know. Maybe one of those bisexual British names — Vivien or Evelyn. Something that wouldn't alarm the police if I had to hand over my license while I was in drag."

"Perhaps he liked Gerald."

"Gerald's a terrible name. I think I like Vivien."

"I'll remind you of that, Rudley, if you ever decide to perform in an evening gown."

The Phipps-Walkers trundled into the lobby with binoculars and cameras.

"So it's confirmed it's another murder, Rudley," Norman said.

Rudley's jaw tensed. "I don't believe that's been established. The investigation is in its early stages."

Norman smiled, showing a pair of buck teeth. "You sound like Detective Brisbois." He lowered his voice. "The scuttlebutt is that Gregoire has already been charged."

Rudley cast a furtive glance around the lobby. "Let's try to keep that to ourselves, Norman, for as long as possible."

"I'm sure they'll realize their mistake soon and let him go," said Margaret.

"I hope so," said Geraldine. "I miss his trout amandine."

"He'll be back before we know it," Margaret said. "In the meantime, try Mr. Cadeau's trout amandine. It's delicious."

"His dishes tend to have a wild flavour." Geraldine shivered. "I hope he's not serving squirrel or rabbit."

"He's not," said Rudley. "I did a head count of the fauna this morning."

"I don't know why Detective Brisbois is being so intransigent," Margaret said.

"Gregoire was the last one to see him alive," Norman said. "As far as we know. And they did quarrel."

"It's all very circumstantial," said Margaret.

"Maybe someone framed him," said Geraldine.

"Maybe the Russian mafia," her husband added.

Rudley crossed his eyes. "What in hell would the Russian mafia be doing around here?"

"The same as the Sicilian mafia, Rudley," Norman said. "Or the Westies or one of the various tongs. It's a quaint backwater with a shifting population and plenty of privacy in which to conduct dirty business without the intense scrutiny of the authorities in the major centres where they are well known."

Rudley looked at him blankly.

"It's common knowledge, Rudley, that the Russians are firmly entrenched in all aspects of organized crime."

Margaret gave Rudley a reassuring pat. "They're really like most of their ilk. It's just that they may be smuggling white slaves or nuclear weapons."

Rudley slammed the register shut. "That is quite concerning, Margaret. However, I can assure you the Russian mafia has not entrenched itself at the Pleasant."

"We'll find out soon enough," said Norman.

Geraldine pointed Norman toward the stairs. "Ta ta, we're off for our nap."

"Wouldn't need a nap," Rudley grumbled, "if they weren't out in the middle of the night harassing the owls and spying on the staff."

The door bumped open.

"Tim!" Margaret held out her arms as Tim crossed the threshold.

He dropped his suitcase and embraced her.

"You should have called."

"I got a ride with the mailman." He took a sheaf of letters from his pocket and dropped them onto the desk.

"How was your vacation?"

"Wonderful. I can't wait to show you my pictures. You'll be green with envy."

"I'll pass on the hug if you don't mind." Rudley backed away.

"Did anything happen while I was gone?"

Rudley picked up the letter opener and slit open an envelope. "The waiter who replaced you was murdered. I think that's about it. Is that about it, Margaret?"

"And Gregoire was arrested and put in jail. We're having a devil of a time getting him out."

Tim considered this. "Then everything is pretty normal. But why is Gregoire in jail?"

"Because they think he killed Gerald."

"Gerald? That's the waiter?"

"Yes," said Rudley. "He was a friend of Gregoire's. He was just filling in for a week or two."

"So Melba could take her harp lessons," Margaret added.

"Why did Gregoire kill Gerald?"

"He didn't," Margaret said. "The police think he did because some of the guests heard them arguing."

Tim shook his head. "I'm sure it's all a misunderstanding. Gregoire argues with everybody. He wouldn't kill anyone. If he did, I'd have been dead a long time ago."

"Tell that to the police."

They turned to see Aunt Pearl weaving down the stairs. She landed at the bottom and made her way to Tim, arms extended. He caught her and gave her a long hug.

"My young Paul Newman. Isn't he the handsomest boy? I saw you getting out of the car from my window. I had to come down right away."

"Not to mention that she heard ice tinkling in a glass a hundred metres away."

"Be nice, Rudley."

"You've probably heard your replacement is tits up and Gregoire's in the slammer."

"I have."

"Well, I know Gregoire," Pearl said. "He wouldn't have done it. If he had, he would have weighed him down with cement and put him further out in the lake. He wouldn't have just dumped him upside down in the swamp."

Tim nodded. "I agree. If Gregoire wanted to kill someone, he would choose a neater method. Like poison. He doesn't like to get his clothes dirty."

Rudley interrupted. "He could have drop-kicked him from the third floor or run over him with the truck. The bottom line is he didn't kill Gerald."

Tim considered this. "Who's doing the cooking?"

"Mr. Cadeau."

"Oh, Mr. Stewed Squirrel and Fricasséed Frogs Legs."

"The man's a cannibal," Rudley muttered. "There's no excuse for victimizing the frogs."

Pearl tugged at Tim's arm. "Tim, I've met someone."

"Tell me more."

"He's adorable. Loads of fun. Kind of jazzy. He's an optometrist. So attentive." She smiled blissfully. "He hangs on my every word."

Tim gave her a peck on the cheek. "I can't wait to meet him." He turned to Margaret. "I'm going to stow my stuff in the bunkhouse, get into my black and whites, and help with lunch."

"It's still your time off, Tim."

"Well, if he wants to, Margaret."

"Rudley."

"Tomorrow's good."

Mr. Harvey entered. He approached the desk, removing his hat. "I hear you've had some trouble. I wanted to offer my condolences."

Margaret smiled. "Thank you, Mr. Harvey."

"I hear they think the man was m-m-murdered," said Harvey. "Terrible."

"Terrible," Rudley muttered.

"If I can do anything to help…"

"We appreciate your concern," Margaret said. "Why don't you join us for lunch — as our guest."

"Good idea," said Rudley. "We'll be serving lunch in about twenty minutes." Rudley took Pearl by the arm. "Pearl, why don't you join Mr. Harvey? If you hop to it, you'll get a nice window seat."

Pearl narrowed her eyes at Rudley, but took Mr. Harvey's arm and steered him toward the dining room.

"Now, Rudley, was that nice? You know she was planning to have lunch with Mr. Lawson."

"Oh, just setting the cat among the pigeons, Margaret. I thought that warty little rat could use some competition."

"I think you're setting Mr. Harvey up for a disappointment."

"He's…" Tim stopped as Margaret and Rudley looked at him expectantly. "That Mr. Harvey gives me the creeps."

Margaret gave Tim a surprised look.

"He's always drifting around the edges," said Tim. "Watching and listening. Doug at the library told me he comes to the book club. He always sits in the back row. Not saying much. Just smiling."

"I think he's just bashful, Tim."

"Doug says he won't give out his telephone number," Tim persisted. "He contacts them by e-mail. If someone asks him a direct question, he changes the subject. They know he's a teacher and that he comes from Michigan and that's about it."

"Maybe he doesn't like to say much because he stutters sometimes," said Margaret.

"Or because he has something to hide."

"Margaret, it's very kind of you to bring me this food." Gregoire's eyes were moist. "I could not have tolerated the menu from Joe's Diner another minute. And this" — he fingered the collar of his orange jumpsuit — "words cannot describe."

"It is a bit loud. I suppose they want to make sure you don't get shot in the forest."

"Believe me, I would not even go into the forest wearing this thing."

"I hope you like the ravioli. It's not as good as yours, of course."

"Compared to Joe's beef stew, it will be ambrosia."

"The guests miss your cooking — although Cadeau is… adequate. They're asking when you'll be back."

"I will be back the minute that ridiculous detective releases me. He knows in his heart I did not kill Gerald." He threw up his hands. "All I know, Margaret, is that I called Gerald to wake him up. He didn't answer the phone so I went to find him and" — he paused and massaged his forehead — "there he was. It was terrible. I cannot describe. Then I was kidnapped and brought here. I can hardly get my brain fixed on that Gerald is gone."

Margaret put a hand on his shoulder. "I know how distressing this is for you, dear." She lowered her voice. "Now, I've come to get you out of here. Rudley and I have consulted with a lawyer. She's going to see if she can work out a bail arrangement with the Crown."

He shook his head emphatically. "I will leave here only if it's free and clear."

"Gregoire" — she fixed him with her warm brown eyes — "principle is all very well and good. But if all it's doing is keeping you in this terrible place for no good purpose…"

"It's for a good purpose."

She eased the ravioli toward him. "Eat this before it gets cold."

He tasted the ravioli, gave a grudging nod of approval. "He's quite good, Margaret. He has a facility for the subtlety of seasonings, which is hard to grasp in a man of otherwise Neanderthal tastes." He paused and lifted a piece of pasta with the fork. "He is not still trying to shoot the squirrels?"

"Rudley's keeping a close eye on that situation. You have to sympathize with Mr. Cadeau in a way. His specialty is authentic North American cuisine."

Gregoire sniffed. "I am sure he is greatly missed in the lumber camps where he learned his trade."

"The guests are raving about his lake trout. They love his cornbread — perfect texture, and of course, quintessential pioneer fare. He did a salad with forest products that even Rudley had to applaud."

He gave her a suspicious look. "I know what you are doing, Margaret. You are trying to appeal to my vanity as a chef."

She sighed. "We just want you back and for this awful business to be over. Mr. Cadeau can fill in adequately and everyone is taken with the novelty. But we want you. We wouldn't expect you to return to work right away, of course. You'll need some time to recover. But we can't leave you languishing in this dungeon, eating Joe's beef stew and wearing that baggy orange coverall."

"It would be more humane to leave us naked." He took another bite. "It is delicious, Margaret, but my appetite is kaput."

She leaned forward. "Gregoire, tell Brisbois what he wants to know. It can't be that bad."

He folded his arms. "It is not anything hideous. But it has nothing to do with Gerald's murder. Once Brisbois realizes that I did not kill Gerald, he will let me go."

She sighed. "You know it often takes a very long time before Detective Brisbois realizes anything."

Chapter Twelve

"I think an original watercolour is an extravagant prize for the pumpkin-carving contest, Margaret."

"It's a small piece, Rudley, hardly more than a study."

"What have you got for the apple bob?"

"Five pounds of Lucille Johnston's hand-dipped chocolates. And for best costumes, a lovely selection of Eva and Mira's maple butters and jams."

"I'd like that one."

"I don't think you're allowed to win anything, Rudley. It would look as if the fix were in."

Aunt Pearl came out of the dining room with Roy Lawson. "Toodle-oo."

"Going out?" Rudley asked.

"We're going to do the town."

"That should take about five minutes."

Roy smiled, displaying a gold incisor.

"We'll probably grab a latte at the hotel, take in the chanteuse at the piano bar, then take a stroll along the pier." Pearl lowered her voice. "Then who knows?" She smirked and grabbed Roy by the arm. "Let's go, Roy."

"She seems to have the old geezer firmly in her clutches," Rudley remarked.

"The old geezer doesn't seem to have any objections."

"It's a veritable match made in heaven."

"Don't be cynical. New love. Remember, Rudley?"

"Ah, yes, Margaret."

Margaret sorted through a sheaf of papers. "Everything is coming together for the Halloween bash. I've got costumes arranged for everyone who didn't bring one. We're going to have a full house." She paused and shook her head. "The professor. He hasn't left his chalet. Hasn't come up for a meal. He must be agoraphobic or an invalid of some sort."

"Perhaps he's both, Margaret. An invalid and an agoraphobic. He never orders anything of substance. He didn't strike me as particularly robust when I signed him in. I thought he might faint before Tiffany got him to the Oaks."

"Yes, he looked rather wan while Lloyd and I were helping him move his things to the High Birches the other day. I think I'll pay him a visit tomorrow. See if I can persuade him to attend the party. I'm sure I can find an appropriate costume. We can't have a guest come to the Pleasant and spend his entire visit sequestered in his cabin eating soup and cheese sandwiches."

"Yes, we can, Margaret, especially one who is so paranoid about being mobbed over a few stanzas."

"He's a professor of literature, Rudley, a sensitive soul."

Rudley gazed off across the lobby. "'Hail to thee, blithe spirit...'"

She clapped her hands. "Rudley, you devil." She gave him a kiss and took off toward the dining room."

Rudley gave himself a pat on the shoulder. "You're a regular ringed-tailed snorter, Rudley."

A paper rustled in the corner. Rudley looked up to see Paul Harvey emerging from the wing chair in front of the mantle.

"Mr. Harvey, I didn't know you'd come in."

Harvey folded his newspaper and tucked it under his arm. "I went up to the village for the early movie. Thought I'd drop in for a glass of wine. You have the best wine cellar in the province."

"Are you all right to navigate back to your spot in the dark?"

"I'm fine, Rudley. It was just one glass." He edged toward the door as he spoke.

"Watch out for the shoals."

"I'll be careful." Harvey smiled. "Good night, Rudley."

"All right. Good night, then."

Harvey left. Margaret returned. She paused to check the flowers on the mantle. "I should take Albert for his walk."

"With his energy level you could trundle him about on a dolly."

"They did say at the shelter he was a calm dog."

"He's practically comatose."

She gave Albert a fond look. "But he's so good-natured."

"He is that."

She slipped behind the desk. "I love this time of day, Rudley. The evening meal winding down. The guests gathering in the drawing room."

"Ah, yes, Margaret, the end of another day. And a good day it's been."

Her brow puckered. "Except that Gregoire's still in jail. On a matter of principle he won't divulge."

"I wish he'd be a little looser in his principles."

"I'm going to talk to Detective Brisbois as soon as he comes back up."

"Back up? I didn't know he was here."

"He is. I just saw him go down the path with Detective Creighton."

Creighton and Brisbois moved along the perimeter of the Pleasant. The night was perfect autumn, mellow and warm, with clouds that drifted and shredded on a light breeze. Leaves crunched under their feet.

"I'm surprised Rudley hasn't sent Lloyd to rake these up," said Creighton.

Brisbois looked at him in surprise. "Why? They look nice. If you come to a country inn in the fall, you expect to be knee-deep in leaves. They're part of the atmosphere."

"They make a lot of noise."

Brisbois considered this. "Yeah, it would be hard to move around quietly. But I suppose with animals always out and about, no one pays much attention."

Creighton chuckled. "That dog Rudley got isn't much, is he?"

"If you want a big easygoing mutt who takes up half the lobby, I'd say he's just about perfect."

They worked their way toward the bunkhouse, skirted the path, and climbed the slope to the wood lot. The lights from the inn twinkled between bare branches. They stood in silence, staring down toward the lake.

"Creepy," said Creighton.

Brisbois did not respond. In spite of the inn and nearby cottages, the place felt deserted. He thought the lake had a different sound in autumn, heavy and foreboding. He missed the swish of the wind through green leaves; the sound of the water lapping against the dock seemed to carry further in summer. It was as if the landscape were giving in to the inevitability of winter. "What was it like that night?"

"A lot like this. Heavy fog packed in early morning."

"This date Gerald had," Brisbois said. "Nobody mentioned seeing a car pick him up."

"No. The Phipps-Walkers just said he took off down the path toward the inn."

"And nobody saw him come home."

"No."

Brisbois frowned. "How do we know he even had a date?"

"He told Trudy he had a date. She said she had a date and he said he did too and gave her a wink."

"Maybe he was just teasing her," Brisbois said.

"The Phipps-Walkers said he was dressed as if he were going out. Red shirt. Leather pants. Lipstick."

"I guess that's going out," said Brisbois. He followed the moon as it slipped out from behind a cloud. "Have you noticed how this time of year the moon starts to look cold?"

"I can't say that I have."

"This time of year would be perfect if you didn't know winter was coming."

"I guess there's a downside to everything."

Brisbois sighed. Creighton didn't have a romantic note in his soul. He turned his attention to the landscape. The inn looked cozy and welcoming. Shadows drifted back and forth across the windows. Margaret might be presiding over a euchre tournament or an evening of charades. She liked all of the old games. He guessed that was why he felt so comfortable at the Pleasant.

Creighton studied him for a moment. "You seem kind of tense, boss."

"I'm fine." Brisbois exhaled sharply. What did he have to be tense about? His wife seemed a little distant these days. Why, he wasn't sure. Maybe it was the new job at the bank, going from part-time to full-time with a promotion. Or maybe it was because their youngest was now away at university. That changed the routine around the house. With the kids away, with him working odd hours as usual, his wife had developed her own social circle. What did he expect her to do? Sit home and knit?

"I hear Miss Miller's coming for the Halloween party," Creighton said. "Maybe she can help us tie up the loose ends."

Brisbois cocked his head to hear a screech owl over Creighton's chatter. He wished Creighton would learn to appreciate silence.

Miss Miller had kept him abreast of her activities since he met her at the Pleasant the summer before last. A few months ago, she had taken leave from her job at the Metropolitan Library, snared an assignment with the *Star*, and set out to travel the world as a feature writer. Her companion, Edward Simpson, had completed his doctorate in Canadian literature and was able to join her. He had received post cards from Hanoi, Shanghai, and most recently, from Outer Mongolia.

Miss Miller had saved his life once. He didn't feel uncomfortable about that. Miss Miller knew that people were apt to get into a fix from time to time and need rescuing. She felt it was her duty to come to their aid.

He thought it would be fun to have Miss Miller as a partner. They'd make a great team — he with his logical detection techniques, she with her wild, and occasionally spot-on, leaps of logic. He glanced at Creighton who was absently snapping off twigs, breaking them into bits, and dropping them at his feet. No one could accuse Creighton of having imagination.

Not that Creighton didn't have some admirable qualities. He was a good sounding board. He didn't have a nerve in his body. Brisbois couldn't think of a cooler head to have around if he were in a jam. He was a bit sarcastic, though. Maybe that's why he was a bachelor.

"Doesn't look as if there's much for us to find here," Creighton said.

"The pathologist found bruise marks on Gerald's legs," Brisbois murmured, "clearly identifiable as handprints. No fingerprints. The assailant was wearing gloves which had a trace of motor oil on them."

"Yeah," said Creighton, "somebody with big hands grabbed Gerald by the legs while the other guy's sitting on his chest suffocating him. Maybe he did that to keep him from flailing around."

Brisbois rubbed his forehead. "Our case against Gregoire would look a lot better if it had been cooking oil."

"And if Gregoire had big hands," said Creighton. "And if the phone logs didn't confirm he'd made that call to the bunkhouse."

"So maybe Gregoire didn't kill him," said Brisbois. "But then whoever did had to know nobody was staying at the bunkhouse except Gerald and Gregoire. And that person had to know pretty much exactly what time Gregoire left to go to the kitchen."

"But that person didn't expect Gregoire to come back down to the bunkhouse. At least not so soon."

"Yeah." Brisbois' ears keened to the lake. "So what does that add up to?"

Creighton shrugged. "Maybe the date was with a guest. Nobody saw anybody pick him up or bring him home because the date was on the property."

Brisbois smiled. "Intriguing possibility." He took out a cigarette and lit it. "Maybe Gregoire isn't talking because he doesn't want to cause trouble for a guest."

"Which means he doesn't think the guest is the guilty party."

"Could be." Brisbois gave Creighton a triumphant look. "See what you can learn by wandering around in the woods?"

"I'll bet we could have come to the same conclusion back at the office."

"Yeah, eventually. After we'd got past trying to find the Rosetta Stone in our notebooks." He started toward the inn. "We'll have to interview everybody again."

"Tonight?"

"No. Tonight we'll go back over our notebooks and see what they said the first time."

Chapter Thirteen

Margaret trundled the tray up to the High Birches and knocked on the door. Adolph opened it a crack.

She gave him her best smile. "Professor, it's Mrs. Rudley. I've brought your lunch." She hustled past him and plunked the tray down on the desk. "One bowl of cream of carrot soup and a whole-grained bun. I've taken the liberty of adding a salad and a nice piece of rhubarb shortcake."

"Oh, I don't know if —"

"Nonsense, you need to keep up your strength. All that reading. Tiffany told me she brought you the complete works of just about everyone in your field."

Adolph glanced at the thick volumes on the bookcase. "She did."

"She has a passion for literature, as you may have guessed. These are her own volumes."

"Yes, it was kind of her to bring them."

"She's a lovely girl." Margaret took Adolph by the arm, steered him toward his tray. "Now, Professor Wyler, I don't want to keep you from your lunch. But I want to make sure you'll be joining us for the Halloween festivities."

"I hadn't thought about it, Mrs. Rudley."

"It's a costume ball with a historical theme. But you really wouldn't have to adhere to the theme. You wouldn't have to dress up at all if you didn't want to. There'll be lots to do."

"Costumes?"

"Yes." Her eyes brightened at his faint show of interest. "We've collected costumes of all sorts for our summer theatre. We have a sailor's outfit for South Pacific and a cowboy for Oklahoma. You could come as a cowboy or a horse." She thought for a moment. "That wouldn't do, of course, unless you could find a partner." She brightened, leaned forward. "How would you like to come as a riverboat gambler?"

"I don't think that's my style."

"Let me think." Her eyes lit up. "I know. Absolutely perfect. I have a mouse's costume from a children's play we did this summer. You could come as a rat from the Great Plague."

"Oh, I don't know."

"It has the most wonderful head. Ears, whiskers, the cutest little mouse nose."

"Mrs. Rudley…"

"Of course you'll come. We can't have you spending your whole time here, sitting inside, reading the Romantic poets, even if you do enjoy them."

He hesitated. "No one would know who I was?"

She looked puzzled, then smiled. "Oh, yes, you don't want to be pestered. Because of your specialty."

"That's right."

"I understand perfectly. I, for one, would be after you all night, begging for quotes from Shelley, demanding insights into the affairs of Lord Byron." She patted him on the shoulder. "Don't worry. Your secret is safe with us."

"I'll think about it, Mrs. Rudley."

"I know you'll say yes."

"Thank you." He let her out and returned to his lunch. He picked up the roll, then put it down. He glanced at the door and realized he had forgotten to lock it. He got up, secured the door, and began to pace.

Mrs. Rudley was a lovely woman. Normally, he would have found her concern touching. Instead, he felt trapped. The idea of spending an evening in a mouse suit made his skin crawl. He would suffocate; the only way to get relief would be to remove his head — which he couldn't do.

He lifted the curtain and peeked out.

Deathly still, apart from the occasional shriek of a jay. The inn was barely visible through the trees. He went back to the desk. Mrs. Rudley had set the soup in an insulated nest. It was still hot. He took a teaspoonful. His hand shook. He grabbed the serviette and dabbed at his chin.

Halloween. He imagined it. Dark and windblown. Menacing steps, their sound distorted by rustling leaves. The tree limbs groaning, muffling his frantic, choking pleas for mercy. He shuddered. No one would be around. Even that strange pair he had seen lurking back of his cabin with their binoculars and cameras would be down at the inn. He imagined the inn packed to the gills with noisy costumed revelers. Nobody would think of him. He might even have trouble getting his supper delivered.

He forced himself to try a piece of the roll. It stuck in his throat, causing him to drop his serviette and beat on his chest to dislodge it. He took a drink of the milk and, gradually, the spasm subsided.

He felt lonely and terrified. He had barely slept. Perhaps, if he slipped a bag of ice cubes inside the mouse suit, he could bear the heat. He checked the small tray in his bar refrigerator. It was half-full. He carried the tray to the sink, filled it, and returned it to the freezer, slopping water across the floor.

He went to the door and checked the lock. Somehow they had found them. They had killed Gerald and they would kill him too. It was just a matter of time.

He picked up the phone. "May I speak to Mrs. Rudley?"

"Speaking."

"I've decided to take you up on your gracious offer of the mouse costume." He paused while she expressed her enthusiastic approval. "Are you sure no one would know I was in that costume?"

She told him it would be their secret. He hung up, feeling relieved. He trusted her. He went back to the table and tackled the soup, spoonful after shaky spoonful.

Brisbois sat down on a bench near the dock and began to thumb through his notes. "Let's sort this out. The Phipps-Walkers and the Sawchucks saw Gerald and Gregoire having an argument around 10:30 in the evening. Gregoire went back into the bunkhouse. Gerald took off toward the inn."

"And no one admits seeing him again."

"Okay." Brisbois flipped a page. "We can rule out Gregory Frasor. He was in the hotel bar in Middleton until 12:15."

"At which time he was thrown out for getting drunk and making an ass of himself. The bartender was gracious enough to call a cab, which delivered him to the Oaks at about 12:40."

"Sparing the paramedics the job of scraping him off a spruce tree." Brisbois waved a hand. "We have the Sawchucks and the Phipps-Walkers and the old dolls at the Elm Pavilion, all of whom I believe when they say they didn't have a date with Gerald."

Creighton laughed. "Hey, I think the Benson sisters would be a lot of fun."

"James Bole was in town attending a performance at the public library. Jazz quartet. He stayed for refreshments and didn't return until 11:30."

"Gerald wasn't his type anyway."

Brisbois ignored him and focused on his notebook. He paused. "What about this guy? Salvadore Corsi. Says he last saw Gerald in the dining room."

Creighton consulted his notes. "Yeah. He went back to his cabin. Says he was expecting a phone call. Business. He's the film director. He said he was here doing a documentary on what rich people do in little places like this. He's shooting some stuff on the horse show, the art colonies, that sort of thing."

"Yeah, okay. Lloyd says he called for a cheese plate and a bottle of wine around nine-thirty. Medical. I think he meant Medoc." Brisbois closed his notebook and put it away. "What do you think about that?"

"I think Lloyd doesn't know much about wine."

Brisbois smiled. "It might mean the gentleman was expecting a guest."

*

"Jim, you're coming to the party, of course." Margaret accosted Devlin as he sprinted into the lobby.

Devlin acknowledged Rudley and Tiffany with a dazzling smile, then turned his attention to Margaret. "Of course I'm coming. I've already sewn my costume."

"Why, Jim, you're a man of extraordinary surprises."

"My mother always said 'Jim, you can do anything you put your mind to.' I'll bet your mother told you that too, Mr. Rudley."

"Of course. The woman taught me everything she knew about the domestic arts." He crossed himself mentally. His mother, fine woman that she was, couldn't sew a button on straight.

"Christopher isn't sure he can come," Tiffany said. "He's been asked to fill in with the string quartet in Lowerton. Their bassist sprained his wrist."

"Tell him to come along when he's finished," Margaret said. "However late, we'll be delighted to have him."

"However late," Rudley murmured.

The door sprang open. A slight, ginger-haired woman with thick glasses sliding down her nose swept into the lobby followed by a slender, tall young man, lugging three suitcases.

Margaret rushed to greet them. "Miss Miller, Mr. Simpson."

Albert bounded up, tail wagging.

Simpson set the luggage down. "Calm down, old chap. Sit."

Albert sat.

"Well, I'll be damned," Rudley said.

"Edward loves dogs," Miss Miller said. She paused and beamed. "I hear you've had another murder."

Salvadore Corsi stared at Brisbois for a long moment, then nodded. "You're right. I was…less than frank. I did see him after I left the dining room. He was here. He asked me not to say anything. Apparently, it's against the rules for an employee to meet privately with a guest. He and the little cook had an argument about it."

"You had a date."

Corsi hesitated. "You could call it that. Why not? I set out a plate of cheese and crackers and a good bottle of wine. I guess that constitutes a date."

"I would say so."

Corsi shrugged. "As it turned out, he was a teetotaler. Fortunately, I had a bottle of ginger ale."

Brisbois searched him with his eyes. "Go on."

Corsi offered a weak smile. "Silly me. I thought this business of 'I hear you do films' was a come-on. As it turned out, he was mainly interested in my business."

"Mainly?"

"Let's just say I didn't get the impression he was averse to sleeping his way to the top."

"Go on."

"We had a pleasant enough evening. He was rather witty, although a bit intense. He had the notion I might be persuaded to do a documentary about female impersonators. With him prominently featured, of course."

"And you weren't persuaded. He got mad. The rest is history."

Corsi shook his head. "No. As a matter of fact, I had the project in mind."

"But not starring Gerald."

Corsi shrugged. "I would have considered him. He had some experience in front of the camera, although he was vague about the details. Hinted his work might be X-rated. I assumed he had done some skin flicks."

"Really?"

"What struck me as odd was that he wanted an assurance he'd be filmed only in makeup. And he indicated he would be using a stage name. I assumed he didn't want his friends and family to recognize him. Rather precious for a man who had done porn."

Brisbois shrugged. "Then what?"

"Then nothing. We talked. He didn't make any overtures. I believe he would have come through if I'd pressured him. I did not.

He stayed until near midnight. I told him I would give him a call once I got back to Toronto. He seemed pleased with that."

Brisbois squared his shoulders. "So you told him that to get rid of him."

Corsi looked surprised. "I was sincere. He did a little audition for me. He was good. If I couldn't have used him in a project, I have colleagues who probably could."

Brisbois looked annoyed. "Why didn't you just tell us all of this before?"

Corsi studied the floor. "I liked Gerald. I was sorry to hear what happened to him. I was shocked. But I didn't want to get involved."

Brisbois tipped his hat forward and massaged the back of his neck. "You didn't want to get involved," he muttered. He looked Corsi square in the eye. "Well, Mr. Corsi, you are involved. Right up to your eyebrows. You could be the last person to have seen him alive." He paused. "Do you know what that means?"

Corsi's mouth drooped. "Surely you don't think I killed Gerald."

"You shouldn't be surprised that I might come to that conclusion."

Corsi sank down onto the bed. "I've heard he was killed early in the morning. Around four."

Brisbois stared at him.

"After my encounter with Gerald" — he moistened his lips — "I went into town. I was feeling a little restless. I couldn't sleep."

"Did anyone see you go?"

"I don't think so. I picked up my car from the parking lot. It's a Honda. Fairly quiet."

"So you killed Gerald on the way home."

Corsi hesitated. "No. I went to the hotel."

Brisbois waved a hand. "Okay, you went to the hotel to drown your sorrows. And?"

Corsi shrugged. "I fell into conversation with a young man. We had a drink together. We stayed at the hotel until closing time. Then we went for a drive up the lake."

"Any witnesses?"

"The bartender. One of your patrolmen. He stopped where we had parked to see if we were having car trouble."

"What time?"

"Just before four-thirty."

"Were you in trouble?"

"Apparently not. He went on his way, although not before asking for my registration."

"What was your friend's name?"

"Troy."

"Troy?"

"I didn't get his last name."

Brisbois paused, pen poised. "And then what? After the officer told you to move along?"

"We drove back to Middleton. We bought coffee at the bait shop on the dock. I dropped him off downtown. I arrived back at the inn at about 6:30." He shrugged. "I drove in. I saw the emergency vehicles parked beside the bunkhouse. I assumed there'd been a break-in. I parked my car and went on to my cottage."

"Did you talk to anyone? Who saw you drive up?"

"Nobody as far as I know. Everybody seemed too busy to notice me."

Brisbois pondered this. "What I don't get, Corsi, is why you just didn't tell us this in the first place. We're all adults. So you spent the night entertaining a series of young men."

Corsi gave Brisbois an injured look. "I hadn't done anything wrong."

"But you thought it might hurt your career if the story hit the newspapers."

Corsi laughed. "Hardly. In my business it's almost a badge of honour." He sobered. "But my wife…"

"Your wife wouldn't understand," Brisbois prompted.

Corsi smiled weakly. "She's my producer."

"So she holds the purse strings."

Corsi shrugged. "Let's say she wouldn't be pleased. Besides, there's my children, my grandchildren to consider."

Brisbois slammed his notebook shut. "You've got to be kidding."

*

Brisbois was still shaking his head as they walked to the car. "I don't know how people like him live with themselves."

Creighton shrugged. "You might not like his style but he's got an ironclad alibi."

Brisbois pushed his hat back. "Even if he didn't, it would be hard to imagine him killing Gerald. Spindly little guy. Must be at least sixty."

Brisbois took a turn onto the dock, walked to the end. Creighton followed.

"Don't jump," said Creighton. "It isn't that bad."

Brisbois gave him an aggrieved look.

"So if it wasn't Corsi and it wasn't Gregoire, then it must have been somebody from outside."

Brisbois took out a cigarette. "They would have had to know when Gerald would be alone."

"They'd have to get that information from somebody at the inn."

Brisbois turned abruptly and headed back up the dock. "I think we're going to a party."

The dining room was empty save for the table by the kitchen. Gregoire, minus his chef's cap, and Tim, immaculate at the end of a long evening, sat around the table with Miss Miller, Mr. Simpson, and the Rudleys.

"I can't believe Detective Brisbois thought you were a murderer, Gregoire," said Miss Miller.

Gregoire bristled. "I don't think for one minute he believed I was a murderer. He was being stubborn because he wanted me to tell him something I did not want to tell him."

"You didn't want to tell him that Gerald had a date with Mr. Corsi."

"That was it," said Gregoire. "That was all. It wasn't important."

Margaret put a hand on Gregoire's shoulder. "Gregoire was trying to protect our reputation. He didn't want to see lurid headlines splashed all over the tabloids: 'Sex Escapade Leads to Murder.' That sort of thing."

Gregoire blushed. "Yes, and I couldn't see that Mr. Corsi would have killed Gerald. He's just a little older guy."

"And he was also trying to protect Gerald's mother," said Margaret.

Gregoire's eyes teared. "I couldn't have her see something like that in the papers. I couldn't have Gerald's lifestyle pushed in her face like that. She was so good to me when I was little. She stood up for me when other kids picked on me. We came to Newcastle from Quebec because my father got a job. The kids thought my accent was funny." He moistened his lips. "And she taught me to cook. My apple pie and rhubarb shortcake are hers. Even after we moved back to Longueuil, she sent me recipes."

"That's very noble of you," said Simpson.

"Is the Crown charging you with obstructing the investigation?" Miss Miller asked.

Gregoire sighed. "Let's say we made a deal. They will not charge me with that and I will not sue them for charging me with murder with such flimsy evidence."

"I'm sorry about the death of your friend," said Simpson.

Gregoire shook his head. "Poor Gerald. He was not a bad person. But he could get into a lot of hot water sometimes. Detective Brisbois is certain he was killed because he was doing something reckless."

"Was he doing something reckless?"

"He was a waiter. Sometimes he worked as a female impersonator. Apart from turning an ankle in his stilettos or tripping over the hem of his evening gown, I cannot see how he was doing anything reckless. But I don't think the detective sees it that way."

"Detective Brisbois can be unsophisticated at times," Margaret said.

"Well," said Miss Miller, "I'm here now."

"Fresh from Outer Mongolia," Tim added.

"It was lovely. Wasn't it, Edward?"

"It was." He cleared his throat. "Stimulating."

"Edward especially liked the yak rides."

"The locals were quite taken with Elizabeth," Simpson said. "They were especially impressed with her willingness to eat all sorts of things."

"Let's just say their culinary arts are different from yours, Gregoire."

Tim relaxed back in his chair. "Do you have a theory about the murder, Miss Miller?"

"Did you say Gerald was murdered between the time Gregoire left for the kitchen and returned an hour later?"

"That's the rumour."

Miss Miller narrowed her eyes. "Then clearly it was an inside job."

Chapter Fourteen

Creighton and Brisbois, in matching clown costumes, sat on a deacon's bench just inside the ballroom door.

"Do you think we're fooling anyone in these outfits?"

"With this nose, my wife wouldn't recognize me."

"I feel like an idiot."

Brisbois shrugged. "So what? These costumes are roomy enough to conceal our weapons. Besides, they're comfortable."

"We could have come as gorillas."

"Just keep smiling and pay attention."

Creighton gave his shoes a disparaging look. "So far, we've witnessed several reels and minuets, a seventy-year-old woman doing the Charleston, and an apple-bobbing contest. The best moment, so far, was when Doreen Sawchuck pinned the tail on Rudley's ass."

"She tripped. The poor old gal has arthritis." Brisbois smiled and nodded as a couple dressed like Sir John A. Macdonald and his wife, Agnes, stopped near them. Sir John's costume included a mask with a prominent nose. "Nice costumes," he said.

They nodded their thanks.

Creighton pulled at his ruff. "You know what Miss Miller would say if she were here?"

"I hate to think."

"She'd say we don't know what in hell we're doing."

Mrs. Macdonald snapped her fan shut. "Miss Miller would never swear, Detective Creighton. Not that Miss Miller is a prude. She simply believes that swearing displays an absence of imagination or a failure to command the vocabulary of our English language. Isn't that right, Mr. Prime Minister?"

"If you say so, Agnes."

Creighton stared, bewildered. Brisbois shook his head, then rose to shake hands. "Miss Miller. Simpson. I heard a rumour you'd be here for Halloween."

She tapped him smartly on the shoulder with her fan. "I wish I could say I was flabbergasted to see you, Detective, but given the idiosyncrasies of the Pleasant..."

"Say no more."

"Shall I fetch you some cider?" Simpson asked his companion.

"Thank you, sir."

"Gentlemen?"

"Nothing for us, thanks."

Creighton waited until Simpson was out of earshot. "So, you haven't snared him yet."

"On the contrary. He's quite well snared."

"I thought you would have been married by now."

She fluttered her fan. "As you may know, Detective Creighton, it's more exciting to hunt without a licence."

Brisbois suppressed a smile.

She folded her fan and sat down on the Queen Anne chair next to Brisbois. "Let's recap your situation, Detective."

He crossed his arms, amiably. "All right."

"You have a man murdered. As yet, you don't know who did it or why."

"I haven't a who yet. I have a pretty good idea about the why."

She leaned toward him. "Do tell."

"The usual reasons, Miss Miller, money, love, revenge."

"That strikes me as simplistic, Detective."

"Well, you know, when you hear hoof beats, think horses not zebras."

She tilted her head. "Obviously, you think the killer may be here tonight."

"Might be."

"Otherwise, you wouldn't be here."

"Dressed like Bozo and Chuckles the Clown," Creighton finished.

"Actually, I like your costumes. Especially the large red shoes." She paused. "You've vetted the guests?"

"Of course."

"Any red flags?"

"You tell me."

She frowned. "I've been here just twenty-four hours, Detective. I haven't had a chance to get to know everyone. Tim seems to find Mr. Harvey suspicious. I must say, he strikes me as oily."

"So does my car mechanic, Miss Miller, but I'm pretty sure he's not a murderer." He paused. "Did you have anyone else in mind?"

She smiled. "Give me a few more days."

Simpson returned with the apple cider.

"We were discussing the recent murder, Edward."

"Shocking," he said. "Terrible for Gregoire." He paused, then said hopefully, "I imagine the detectives have the matter well in hand."

She beamed. "Edward, dear, of course they don't."

Napoleon, aka Gregory Frasor, staggered across the ballroom to the buffet. He snared a glass of punch and lumbered over to the mouse who stood in the corner, balancing a plate of canapés. "Let me guess" — he waved a hand in the mouse's face — "you're the guy who chases the birds."

The mouse froze.

"No. You're too short." Napoleon snapped his fingers. "I've got it. You're the old guy I play poker with."

The mouse turned away.

Napoleon grabbed a fuzzy ear and pulled.

The head came off. The plate shattered on the floor.

"Professor!" Margaret ran toward him and grabbed the mouse's head from Napoleon, who was waving it like a captured flag. "Let me help you." She stuck the head back onto Adolph who had shrunk back against the wall and led him into the hallway.

Miss Miller turned toward Simpson. "Did she say 'professor'?"

Simpson nodded. "That was rather immature of Napoleon. The gentleman seems distraught."

"I don't remember seeing him before." Miss Miller looked to the detectives, who exchanged glances and shrugged.

"He's a bit of a recluse," whispered Tim who had come to refill the punch bowl. "Doesn't leave his cabin as a rule."

Frasor took a slug of punch and set out to pursue the mouse into the hallway.

Rudley seized him by the shoulder. "Now, Mr. Frasor , perhaps you'd care to take part in the ring toss." He steered Frasor toward the opposite side of the room. "Right this way."

"It's been a splendid party, Rudley."

Rudley glanced around. The party had dwindled to a few stray souls. "Thank you, Mr. Bole. I hope the guests had a good time."

"A good time, as always." Bole tipped his hat. "Sorry about the accident."

Rudley put a hand tenderly on his right buttock. "All in a day's work.

Margaret waved to Mr. Bole as he left. "You were a good sport about that, Rudley."

"I'm just grateful she didn't have more than a tack in her hand." He looked around. "I take it Tiffany bribed the parents to take the last of the children."

"They're all gone, Rudley. I think Tiffany went out back with Lloyd. They were going to light the jack-o'-lanterns and take some pictures for the scrapbook."

"Fine idea."

"I guess Christopher isn't going to make it."

"Pity."

"And Jim didn't show up. I thought he was keen."

"The man's such an airhead, Margaret, he probably forgot the date."

Detectives Brisbois and Creighton emerged from the ballroom.

"I wondered where you clowns had gone," said Rudley.

"Funny, Rudley." Brisbois turned to Margaret. "Lovely party, Margaret."

"Any new ideas on Gerald's murder?" she asked.

"Nothing in particular. Just a few things jiggling around."

"With any luck they might run into each other by spring," Rudley murmured.

"Be nice, Rudley."

The detectives left. Mr. Frasor teetered out of the ballroom.

"I guess I've overstayed my welcome." He looked back over his shoulder, almost losing his balance. "Looks as if I'm the last one out."

"I take it you had a good time."

"I had a wonderful time, Mrs. Rudley. So good, I think I'll come back next year." He grinned. "Maybe sooner."

"Would you like an escort back to your cabin?"

"No, I'll be fine, Rudley. I could get there in my sleep."

"Good night, then." Rudley turned to Margaret. "Did the mouse ever come back?"

"I'm afraid not. I'll have to go down in the morning to apologize. I had no idea anyone would tamper with his head. I forgot to tell him it zippered on. I did it up for him but he wouldn't stay."

Rudley stretched. "Well, apart from that, a good evening was had by all, I would say."

"Indeed." She sighed. "I suppose we should go in and package up the leftovers."

He put an arm around her. "Take a break, Margaret. Tiffany and Lloyd will be back in soon. They'll want a snack. Tim and Gregoire are still in the kitchen. They'll want something, too. We might even get Miss Miller and Mr. Simpson back for a nightcap."

"They went upstairs rather early."

"Something about a big nose being seductive." He smiled and turned to show her his profile. "I've always believed that myself."

She waved him off. "Oh, Rudley."

"Let me get you a glass of wine and we'll…"

Rudley's words were lost in two sharp cracks, sounding out in rapid succession.

Rudley stiffened.

Margaret gasped. "Do you know what that sounded like?"

"Yes, Margaret." He grabbed her and pulled her down behind the desk.

Tim reached for a walnut meringue. "I'm glad the guests didn't scarf all of these."

Gregoire surveyed the sandwiches. "We have enough left over for some bedtime snacks. The children demolished everything I prepared for them." He snapped to attention. "What was that?"

Tim reached for a serviette and wiped his fingers. "One of our drunken patrons must have set off a firecracker."

"It sounded like a very big firecracker."

Tim reached for another meringue, then recoiled at the clank of metal on metal. "I think something just hit the flagpole."

Gregoire grabbed Tim's arm. "That was not a firecracker."

"You're probably right." Tim dropped the meringue and dove under the table.

Gregoire joined him.

"It's probably one of the boys from town," Tim said. "Maybe that idiot who murdered the pumpkins last year."

"You mean tipping cows is now out of fashion?"

"Guess so."

"What should we do?"

"Call the police."

Gregoire glanced toward the phone. "Which one of us is going to put our head over the table?"

"How about the short one with the tall hat."

Gregoire gave Tim a sour look.

They were quiet for a moment, then Tim said, "I think Tiffany and Lloyd are out back."

They scrambled together for the phone.

Margaret winced. "There's another."

"I know." Rudley pulled her closer.

"What should we do?"

"I'm not sure." He paused, straining to listen. "I wonder where Brisbois and Creighton are."

"Probably halfway back to town."

"Of course." He flinched as another report split the air, followed by a metallic ping. "I think he got the flagpole."

A door down the hall burst open. Light, rapid footsteps came up the stairs and advanced toward the desk.

Rudley grabbed an ornamental door stopper. "Get ready, Margaret."

"Mr. Rudley, where are you?"

"Tiffany, get in here."

She gasped. "Mr. Rudley, are you behind the desk?"

"Don't advertise the fact. Just get in here."

She toppled in beside him.

"What in hell is going on?"

"I was out in the back yard with Lloyd," she whispered. "We were trying to decide how to arrange the pumpkins for the photographs. We thought we'd put them against the tall grass beside the bench."

Margaret's voice rose an octave. "Is Lloyd all right?"

The door banged open again. Footsteps pounded down the hall.

"Yoo hoo."

"Lloyd." Margaret waved a hand over the desk.

Lloyd ducked in beside her.

She touched his cheek, then recoiled. "Lloyd, what's that on your face?"

"Someone shot his jack-o'-lantern," said Tiffany.

"It was first-rate too," said Lloyd. "Round like a marble and same colour all around."

"Was anyone else out there?" Rudley rasped.

"Mr. Bole came by, then he was gone."

"Where?"

"I guess to his cottage. He said, 'Is that the jack-o'-lantern that won first prize?' I said yes and he went on."

"Somebody's got to do something." Rudley popped his head over the desk. His eyes darted across the lobby to the unlocked door. He ducked as another shot rang out.

"That one sounded close," said Lloyd.

"Albert hasn't even opened his eyes." Rudley lunged for the phone and dragged it in behind the desk. He stopped to catch his breath, then dialed 911. "Wood Lake Road. The Pleasant Inn." He paused. "Why, I resent that, miss. It's nothing to laugh at. Somebody's shooting at us. What? All right." He hung up. "Tim's already called in from the kitchen."

"I hope he's all right. Is Gregoire with him?"

"We didn't get that chatty, Margaret."

"Bring the phone around, Rudley. If he sees it stretched over the desk, he'll know we're here."

He scrambled to the task. He could hear wood splintering as he plastered himself to the side of the desk. "That better not have been the porch spindles."

"We can replace the spindles." Margaret pulled on his arm. "See if you can wake Albert and coax him in here."

"I don't think whoever it is will bother shooting him, Margaret. He looks dead already."

"Maybe we should lock the front door," Tiffany said.

Rudley hesitated. "Better not. In case someone needs to take cover."

"The police will be here soon," said Margaret.

They sat shoulder to shoulder, staring at the back of the desk. Rudley's watch sounded loud against the silence.

Rudley started. "What's that?"

"What?"

"I heard steps on the gravel."

"Maybe a raccoon," said Lloyd.

"Damn big raccoon." Rudley hitched back against the wall, strained to see through the window. His view was obstructed by a settee. "Where are the damned police?"

"They were probably several miles away when the call went out, Rudley."

Another shot creased the air, followed by a flurry of steps down the staircase.

"What's going on around here?"

"Pearl," Rudley hissed, recognizing the voice, "get in here."

Pearl peeked in behind the desk, her mouth formed into a surprised O. "What's everybody doing here?"

"Those were gun shots, Pearl."

"I know they're gun shots. I thought they were coming from the television."

"I'm afraid not."

"They aren't shooting at us, are they?"

He gave her a stricken look. "He, Pearl. I'd hate to think there's more than one. And I don't think he's being particular. So far, he's destroyed Lloyd's pumpkin and probably hit a flagpole, a tree, perhaps a canoe, the veranda, or the porch spindles." He flinched as a bullet flinted off something hard. "And perhaps a rock."

The shot was followed by a patter up the steps and onto the veranda. The door opened. Rudley peeked out to see a figure in a parrot mask poised uncertainly in the doorway.

"Norman get in here and close the door."

Phipps-Walker approached and stopped in surprise when he saw the group huddled behind the desk.

"Keep your head down," said Rudley. "Didn't you hear the gun shots?"

"I did. I thought they were firecrackers at first."

"Did you see anybody out there?"

"No."

"Where were the shots coming from?"

"Up on the rise, I think. I didn't pay much attention. I was down at the Elm Pavilion, showing the sisters my costume. They had the television cranked up."

"Did you see what he was shooting at?"

"Couldn't tell. One of the bullets hit something by the dock. Another one ricocheted off one of those big rocks and hit the cast-iron flower pot."

Margaret gulped. "Norman, how can you be so calm?"

He thought for a moment. "I didn't think he was shooting at me."

"I doubt if he was taking pains to miss you, Norman."

"I think I hear a car," said Tiffany.

A few minutes later, they heard steps on the veranda. After a long pause, the door burst open. Someone shouted, "Police!"

Rudley waved a hand over the desk. "It's Rudley."

"Come up slowly. Keep your hands where I can see them."

Rudley and the others stood in unison, hands reaching for the ceiling.

The officer's eyes widened. "You must have the whole inn in there, Rudley."

"Someone was shooting at us, you idiot."

The officer gave him a reproachful look. "How many shots?"

"Eight at least. Perhaps nine. Are you all they sent?"

The officer scanned the lobby. "We've got officers around the inn. Where did the shots come from?"

"From the woods up on the rise," said Phipps-Walker.

"Okay." The officer paused. "We've got someone out there who says you people know him." He stepped to the doorway and motioned with one hand.

Two officers entered with a bedraggled pirate between them.

Tiffany's eyes widened. "Christopher."

"So you do know him?"

"It's Christopher Watkins," she said. "Christopher, what happened?"

He gulped. "I was trying to surprise you, Tiffany. I was just coming into the dock when a bullet hit my boat."

"We found him hanging onto the dock by his fingertips," the officer said with a smirk.

"Hell of a time to be out on the lake," Rudley said.

"I had no idea it would take me so long to row down from Middleton."

"Well, don't stand there dripping on the dog." Rudley turned to the dining room door where Tim and Gregoire hovered, wide-eyed. "Gentlemen, could you get the man something to wear?"

The officer waved everyone back toward the desk. "Stay away from the windows. Are the other doors locked?"

"The side door is." Rudley looked to Lloyd.

"Back door too," Lloyd said.

"Good." The officer looked around. "Anybody else in here?"

"The guests are in their quarters," Rudley replied, "except for Norman here. They're either deaf or getting very jaded."

"Okay, you," he said, pointing to Rudley, "dim down the lights." He motioned to one of the other officers. "We're going to check the rooms."

The officers returned a few minutes later. "Everybody upstairs is accounted for. They thought you had your television revved up but didn't have the heart to complain. The young couple" — he grinned — "Miss Miller and Simpson were otherwise occupied."

"It had something to do with his nose," said Margaret.

The officer looked befuddled. "Stay put." He started toward the door.

"You aren't leaving us," said Tiffany.

"He could come through the door any minute and mow us down, one by one," Lloyd added.

The officer put up a reassuring hand. "Relax. Officer Owens has volunteered to station himself outside your door."

"How very brave of him," said Tiffany. She turned to Christopher. "Christopher, don't drip on the desk."

*

Brisbois and Creighton pulled up at the turnoff to the Pleasant and radioed the patrolmen. "Anything yet?"

"We pulled a skinny pirate out of the lake. Otherwise, negative."

"Where are you positioned?"

"We've got four guys up in the woods, one at the front door, one at the back door, and two checking out the cottages."

"Hear anything?"

"No more shots since we got here."

"Okay. We've got a helicopter on the way. We'll light up the woods."

"Acknowledged."

"Be careful."

"Will do." He paused. "These folks are crazy, you know."

"Acknowledged." Brisbois took the keys from the ignition. "We'll walk in from here."

Creighton reached into the back seat for their Kevlars.

Brisbois waved the Kevlar off. "We'll stay close to the lake, keep behind the big trees."

"You watch and I'll listen."

They drew their guns.

The staff and guests sat along the wall on benches and chairs pulled into the hallway, balancing cups of coffee and plates of leftovers.

"I hope the ladies at the Elm Pavilion are all right," said Margaret.

"They've probably fallen asleep in front of a Hitchcock film," Rudley said.

"I'm sorry about your jack-o'-lantern, Lloyd," Margaret said. "You didn't even get a photograph."

"It was terrible," Tiffany said. "Gouts of pumpkin flesh… I imagine the shrubs are plastered with it."

"I don't understand why anyone would want to take pot shots at the Pleasant," Christopher remarked.

"The way things are going, I wouldn't be surprised if someone dropped a bomb on us," Rudley said.

Margaret looked up in horror as the helicopter passed over.

Brisbois and Creighton paused beside the Low Birches.

Brisbois' radio crackled. "Brisbois," he said. "Got something?"

"Sprained ankle. Semple stepped in a hole."

"Well, damned to hell." Brisbois switched the radio to his left hand, took out a package of cigarettes, fumbled one into his mouth, then handed a package of matches to Creighton.

"I thought you were trying to cut down, boss."

"I didn't ask for a health lecture. Just light the damn thing. No," he said into the radio, "I don't want paramedics going up there. He can walk on one leg, can't he?"

"Sure he can."

"I'll have an ambulance meet us in front of the inn."

"Affirmative. Watch your step if you're coming up here."

"Acknowledged." Brisbois signed off, turned to Creighton. "I wish I could figure out what was going on."

Creighton gave him a slap on the back. "Aw, you always say that when we come up here."

"Just watch your step."

The ambulance screamed up to the Pleasant.

"Now we have an ambulance," said Rudley. In spite of Margaret's protests, he got up and went to the door. He flung it open, catching Owens, who was on his way down the steps. "What's that thing doing here?"

"One of the officers stepped in a hole in the woods."

"I suppose that's better than being shot."

Owens held up his hand. "Mr. Rudley, please go inside and lock the door."

"What about the guests in the cottages?"

"We're working our way around."

"One of the Benson sisters could have had a heart attack."

Owens sighed and got on his radio. "Richards, have you got to the old ladies in the Elm Pavilion?" He listened, then signed off. "Richards says they're watching *The Attack of the Killer Tomatoes.*" He gave Rudley a beseeching look. "Please cooperate, Mr. Rudley."

"Oh, all right." Rudley ducked back in and locked the door.

"What's wrong, Rudley?"

"One of the officers stuck his big flat foot in a hole."

Pearl shook her head. "You don't have any luck, do you, Rudley? I don't think I've spent three days in a row here without seeing flashing lights and hearing sirens."

"Would you like a sandwich, Mr. Rudley?"

"No, thank you, Tiffany."

"Salmon with dill pickle on whole wheat," said Lloyd, "with a little dollop of Dijon mustard. And chocolate cake, three layers with jam filling in."

"I'll have a small piece of chocolate cake with the jam filling in," said Rudley. He sagged back against the wall, defeated.

"Buck up," said Pearl.

"It's not your fault, dear," said Margaret. "These things happen."

"People roaming around taking potshots at us isn't just one of those things, Margaret."

"I'm sure it was just one of the local boys who'd had too much to drink."

He gave her a morose look. "I don't think our luck's that good, Margaret."

Brisbois stood, hands in pockets, hat pushed back. "Does your ankle hurt, Semple?"

Semple blinked away drops of sweat. "Quite a lot, sir."

Brisbois turned to the uniformed sergeant. "Any shell casings?"

"We've found a couple."

"Anything else?"

"There's some partial footprints in that boggy area over there. They don't look much good though."

Semple groaned.

"Maybe we'd better get him down to the ambulance," said Creighton.

"In a minute." Brisbois leaned down to look at Semple. "You're all right, aren't you?"

Semple hugged his ankle. "Yes, sir."

"I want to take a quick look at those footprints."

The sergeant led him to the site and pointed. Brisbois hunkered down. "Looks as if his foot slipped in the mud. Kind of squashed out. Not much tread." He stood up. "Rope it off for Sheffield. Get him up here as soon as we're sure the area is secure. I guess we'd better get Semple looked after."

The radio crackled.

"We've got a little guy up at the High Birches. Looks like he passed out. I think the gunshots scared the crap out of him."

"Are you sure he didn't take a bullet?"

"Don't look like it. He's just lying here in this little fuzzy grey suit. Whiskers and everything."

Brisbois turned to Creighton. "Professor Wyler. The guy in the mouse costume. They found him passed out." He turned back to the radio. "Get the paramedics to take a look at him."

They returned to where Semple sat gritting his teeth.

"Okay." Creighton leaned down. "Put your arm around my shoulder, bud, and we'll have you out of here in no time."

Brisbois took the other side. By the time they reached the inn, he was sweating. The paramedics loaded Semple into the ambulance bay.

"Did you check out the mouse?"

"Yeah, he's okay. He couldn't get his head off. Got too hot and passed out. He wouldn't let us take him in the ambulance." The paramedic grinned. "Maybe we should set up an aid station here."

"That's not funny."

"I thought it was kind of funny," said Creighton. "It would save all the 911s. They could just step outside and ring the dinner bell."

Brisbois glared at him.

Creighton chuckled. "This place is one giant screw-up."

Brisbois wheeled on him. "Margaret and Rudley are trying to run a nice place. Nothing that's happened is their fault."

Creighton narrowed his eyes. "Why is it always Margaret and Rudley?"

"What should I call them?"

"How about the Rudleys?"

Brisbois was about to respond when his radio crackled.

"Brisbois, you'd better get down here."

The officer directed Brisbois with his flashlight. "We missed him the first time around. No lights on in the cottage. We figured whoever was staying here was still up at the inn."

"I guess you could miss him in the dark." Brisbois caressed his cigarettes. "He's in the bushes beside the door. Keys are a couple of feet away. Porch light's on. So he had his keys out, probably just about to put them in the lock when he gets shot and topples into the bushes. Even with the porch light on, somebody had to be a damned good shot. Maybe he had an infrared scope."

"With all the shots whizzing around, maybe this guy just got unlucky."

"Could be. Or somebody wants us to think that way. Get the forensics guys down here post-haste." Brisbois turned to Creighton. "What do we know about this guy?"

Creighton flipped open his notebook and leaned toward the porch light. "If the guy matches the cottage, it's Gregory Frasor from Hamilton." He took a peek at the body. "Napoleon suit. Yup, that's Frasor. In a nutshell? Forty-year-old computer geek. Divorced. Sort of an aging frat boy. Yuck, yuck and all that. Pays his taxes. No criminal record. Came here because he heard the Halloween party was good and the food was great. Said one of his friends was here a couple of years ago and loved it."

Brisbois gave the body a long look. "Well, I hope he had a good time."

Chapter Fifteen

Rudley leaned over the desk, staring gloomily at the mantle. "Seems familiar, doesn't it, Margaret? Bodies all over the place. Brisbois ensconced in my office."

"I'm afraid so, Rudley."

"I'm sorry about Gerald, but I can't say I regret that Frasor won't be back."

She sighed. "He was a bit boisterous, lacking in the social graces, but he was harmless."

Rudley sprawled across the desk, wrapping his head in his hands. "You're right, Margaret. Nobody deserves to die, however unpleasant."

The laundryman came up the steps and stopped in front of the desk.

Rudley raised his head. "What in hell are you doing here?"

"I went to the rear door to deliver your linens, Mr. Rudley, and guess what I found?"

"A doorknob."

"Be nice, Rudley."

The laundryman smiled. "Now, now, Mr. Rudley. The door was locked. That's what I found."

Rudley dragged himself off the desk. "Damn."

"I'm sorry," Margaret said. "There's been so much going on."

"Yes," the laundryman said. "I heard you'd had some trouble here last night. Something about someone shooting up the Pleasant."

"Bad news travels fast," said Rudley.

"I assumed it was someone you do business with," the laundryman said. "Due to your charming personality."

Rudley pressed his lips together as Margaret shot him a warning look.

"After you," he said to the laundryman.

"I'm glad you could see me early," Christopher said. "I need to get to my office. I have appointments."

Creighton yawned. "Doesn't seem early to us. We've been up all night."

Brisbois glanced at his notes. "This won't take long. I just need to review your statement."

"Of course." Christopher sat in the chair beside Rudley's desk, his wrists dangling out of the sleeves of one of Gregoire's uniforms.

"You said you were coming across the lake, in a rowboat, dressed like a pirate to surprise Tiffany."

Christopher looked aggrieved. "I should have driven."

"Or taken a motor boat."

"Part of the problem was, I'm not that good at navigating the lake. I got a late start. I didn't realize it would take that long to row in from town."

"What time did you arrive at the inn?"

"As I said, it was about a quarter to one when I saw the light at the end of the dock."

"Did you hear the shots as you approached?"

"I heard several explosions. Perhaps seven or eight. The first two were almost simultaneous. You know, pft-pft, then bang, bang, bang, bang, etcetera. I thought it was fireworks from the party. I remember looking and wondering why I didn't see the display."

Brisbois paused, pen poised. "Pft-pft. You mean pft-pft, like two different guns?"

Christopher thought for a moment. "I'm not sure. It was as if the first two shots overlapped. Sort of as if the echoes blended. The other shots were distinct. Bang, bang, bang, and so on. Or perhaps I just wasn't registering what I was hearing at first. I can't say I was paying much attention to my surroundings at that point. I was focusing on manoeuvring the boat into the dock. I was about twenty feet out when something hit my boat. I jumped."

"What next?"

"I swam in, then hung onto the edge of the dock until I saw the police cruiser."

"Then you felt it was safe to come out."

"Yes. And I hadn't heard any more shots after the one that hit my boat."

"Where were the shots coming from?"

"From the woods behind the inn." Christopher shook his head. "I'm sorry I can't be more specific. I'm not very good at noticing things."

Brisbois raised his brows. "Do you have any theories?"

Christopher looked at him, surprised. "I assume the shooter was some inebriated Neanderthal. Too bad that man, Frasor, had to pay for his idiocy."

"Okay." Brisbois jotted a few notes. "As you were rowing over here, did you notice any cars on the road? Traffic on the lake?"

Christopher wrinkled his brow. "I thought I saw pinpoints of light on the water quite a long way up when I was out in the middle of the lake, but nothing came my way." He shrugged. "It was probably just moonlight on the water."

"Do you know what time that was?"

"Sometime just before midnight, I think."

Creighton laughed. "You did take a long time to get here."

Christopher blushed. "I lost my bearings. I almost pulled into the Water's Edge by mistake."

"It's easy to get lost on the water." Brisbois checked his notes. "Anything else?"

"I don't think so."

"Okay. You have our card. If you think of anything, please contact us."

After Christopher left, Brisbois tipped his chair back and sorted through his notes. "So what have we got? Everybody was at the party until midnight, except the Benson sisters who were yucking it up over at the Elm Pavilion, throwing popcorn at a B-movie. Mr. Bole returned to his cottage, the Pines. Didn't see or hear anything on the way down."

"The Pines. Three cottages from the Oaks."

"Yeah. Norman Phipps-Walker went down to take some treats to the Benson sisters and show off his costume. Amazon parrot. Saw nothing on the way down. Heard what he thought were firecrackers. Left the Elm Pavilion. By the time he got halfway to the inn, he decided what he was hearing were gunshots. However, he didn't panic because he assumed they weren't shooting at him."

Creighton grimaced. "He might have been wrong, but he was lucky."

"Tiffany and Lloyd were out behind the inn. The pumpkins got it first. They're certain the shot came from above and directly behind them."

"According to Rudley, the flagpole was next."

Brisbois nodded. "So the shooter didn't stand in one spot and blast away. He had to be moving across the rise and west, shooting, until he came to an angle from the dock. He got Christopher's boat on the starboard side."

"Unless there was more than one person shooting," Creighton said. "Which makes sense. The last shot that anyone heard hit the boat. But Frasor's cottage is west of the dock."

Brisbois nodded. "He had to have been hit earlier." He flipped through his notes. "We have some pretty exact reports about what got hit — the pumpkins, the flagpole, the urn, the boat, the porch spindles, the rock. The two shots that were fired almost simultaneously, one hit the pumpkins, the other must have hit Frasor."

"So he was hit right away," Creighton said. "Bang-bang, then bang, bang, bang…"

"Pft-pft, bang, bang, bang," Brisbois murmured. "There was more than one shooter." He dropped his notebook onto the desk and thumbed through it. "Frasor took a clear shot to the head, the mouse fainted, the flagpole got dinged, the jack-o'-lantern bought the farm, the boat sunk, the flower pot's got a new dent, and Semple sprained his ankle."

"A good time was had by all."

Brisbois turned a page. "Last year someone pumped the pumpkin patch full of lead."

"Yeah, but that was with a shotgun."

"They never got any leads on that."

"Nope. That same night somebody wrecked a stop sign and shot up a couple of outdoor toilets."

Brisbois shook his head. "Occupied?"

"The report doesn't say."

"If they were occupied, it shows a certain degree of recklessness." Brisbois closed his notebook and tucked it into his pocket. "It's going to be a long day. We've got to interview all the guests again. Revisit everybody's background."

"What's next, boss?"

Brisbois smiled. "I think we'll lock that door and catch a two-hour nap."

"That's the best idea I've heard in a long time."

By ten o'clock, the breakfast rush was over. Miss Miller and Simpson had pulled two tables together and were conducting an animated conversation with the Rudleys and staff. Paul Harvey entered the lobby and paused in the dining room doorway. Margaret saw him, then stood and beckoned him over.

"Mr. Harvey, would you like to join us for brunch?"

He smiled and sidled to the chair she indicated. "Thank you. Actually, I've had my breakfast. I'm on my way to Middleton. I wanted to drop by and thank you again for the lovely party." He waved a hand toward the window. "I noticed when I came up you have a police cruiser parked at the side."

"Someone was shot at the Oaks last night," said Tim.

Harvey's jaw dropped. "Oh, no, the professor!"

"No, it was Mr. Frasor."

Harvey frowned. "I didn't hear any gunfire."

"You were probably home by then, Mr. Harvey," said Margaret. "You wouldn't have heard anything from there."

Harvey shook his head. "No, nothing at all."

Aunt Pearl entered at that moment, Roy Lawson trailing after her.

Harvey jumped up and stuttered, "Miss Dutton."

"Mr. Harvey."

"Why don't you sit here? I was just leaving."

"We can get another chair," Margaret protested. "At least have a cup of coffee."

"Really, I must be getting along. I have things to do." He smiled. "Thank you."

They watched him walk away.

"Mr. Harvey always seems so unsettled," Margaret said.

"Anyone with a brain in his head would feel unsettled coming into this madhouse, Margaret," said Rudley.

"He must get lonely over there," Margaret said. "He's been coming here rather frequently lately."

"He makes me shudder," said Gregoire. "So quiet, with his eyes flickering over everything. Like those little house finches."

"And always smiling," said Tim.

"He could be cured of that if he spent a little more time around here," said Rudley.

"Aren't we in a grand mood this morning?" said Pearl.

"Sorry, Pearl. I tend to be down in the mouth the morning after a murder."

"Don't mind him," Pearl told Roy, who was staring myopically at the tablecloth. "He takes these things hard."

Miss Miller leaned across the table. "Why would Mr. Harvey think it was the professor who had been shot?"

"Well, the professor was signed into the Oaks originally. Mr. Harvey wouldn't have known he moved." Margaret paused, frowned. "Although I'm not sure how he would know he had signed into the Oaks in the first place."

Tiffany entered the dining room at that moment, waving a note.

"Mrs. Rudley."

"Yes, dear."

"Mr. Devlin called. He wanted to apologize for missing the party."

"Did you tell him we barely missed him?"

Tiffany ignored Rudley. "He had a problem with his boat. He said he spent hours trying to fix it."

"Only to find it had run out of gas," Rudley murmured.

"He wanted to stop by and see you but he won't have time. He's leaving first thing Friday morning for Portland. Apparently, he has all sorts of things to do before then," Tiffany continued. She paused to check her notes. "He wanted you to know he's going directly from Portland to Toronto, then on to Marrakesh...."

"Best news I've heard in ages," Rudley muttered.

"He'll pop by as soon as he returns," Tiffany finished.

"Into every life some rain must fall," said Tim. As Rudley glowered, he headed for the kitchen, whistling.

Brisbois brought his chair forward with a thump, jolted awake by a hammering on the door. Where in hell was he? The cobwebs cleared when he saw Creighton stretched out on the couch, his hat over his face. He gave his colleague a swat on the leg. "Get up, sunshine. Somebody's at the door."

Creighton swung his legs over the edge of the couch. "What time is it?"

Brisbois looked at his watch. "A quarter to eleven. Damn." He straightened his tie, brushed his hair back, and opened the door.

Miss Miller stood in the doorway. Simpson hovered at her shoulder.

"Detective Brisbois." She swept past him. "We must talk."

"We must?" He started to protest, but she had already ensconced herself on the corner of the desk.

Simpson shrugged apologetically.

"Detective Creighton."

He bowed. "Miss Miller."

"You've been going about your investigation the wrong way."

Brisbois smiled. "We usually do, Miss Miller. As you know, it's our modus operandi."

"Something bigger is at play."

"I see."

"You've postulated Mr. Frasor's death was an accident."

He shrugged. "You tell me."

"I don't think it was an accident."

"Are you suggesting someone was trying to kill Mr. Frasor?"

"I'm not sure if Mr. Frasor was the intended victim."

He raised his brows.

"Have you taken a good look at Mr. Harvey?"

"Harvey?"

"Yes. He had opportunity. He left the party early, before the shooting started."

"He's an older man. He probably didn't want to be out on the lake in the middle of the night."

"Or he didn't want to be around when the bullets started bouncing off the flagpole."

Brisbois contemplated this for a moment. "You're postulating Mr. Harvey didn't do the shooting, but he knew it was about to happen?"

"Perhaps."

Brisbois spun around to face Simpson. "What do you think, Simpson?"

"I try not to, Detective."

Brisbois turned back to Miss Miller. "Okay, let's go along with your theory for the moment. What is there about Mr. Harvey that makes you think he was involved? For instance, where's his motive?"

"I don't know that. Not yet. But what do we know about this man?"

"He's a retired schoolteacher."

"Sounds pretty suspicious," Creighton chuckled.

Brisbois smiled. "Great reports from all sources. Coached the drama club. Was active in Cubs and T-Ball. He came here a year ago. Since then, he's joined the reading club at the library and he started the orchid society."

Miss Miller frowned. "Edward is a member of the orchid society. He has huge Orchidaceae."

Creighton suppressed a smirk. "I think Harvey's are smaller. He specializes in the wild varieties."

Miss Miller erased his smile with a steely look. "Orchids aside, he did leave the party early and came around early this morning, ostensibly to thank the Rudleys for the party. Why didn't he just telephone?"

"He did say he was on his way to the village," said Simpson.

"He pretended he didn't know what happened last night," said Miss Miller.

Brisbois shrugged. "He probably didn't, Miss Miller. His place is up the lake. He wouldn't have seen anything and probably couldn't have heard the shots."

"He asked about the police cars out front, and when he was told there had been a shooting at the Oaks, he said: 'Oh, no, the professor.' And Tim said: 'No, it was Mr. Frasor.'" She leaned forward, triumphant. "Now, why would Mr. Harvey assume the professor had been the victim?"

Brisbois thought for a moment. "Professor Wyler was originally signed in at the Oaks."

"But how would Harvey know the professor was at the Oaks in the first place?"

Creighton yawned and straightened his jacket. "Wouldn't be that hard, Miss Miller. Mr. Harvey comes and goes around here. The staff has been trotting three meals a day to the professor. Harvey may have heard somebody mention the Oaks at some point in the connection with the professor and assumed he was still there."

Brisbois nodded. "It's not that difficult to figure out what's going on around here." He shrugged. "Look at what you've been able to find out."

"But why would anyone want to shoot Frasor? He struck me as nothing more than an overgrown kid."

"That seems to be the general opinion," Brisbois said. "But, at this point, we don't know if anyone was trying to shoot him."

"Then perhaps they were trying to kill Professor Wyler."

"There doesn't seem to be any reason anybody'd want to kill him either, Miss Miller. Or anyone else at the Pleasant for that matter."

"Except perhaps Rudley," Creighton said.

"The professor is rather eccentric," Miss Miller went on. "Prior to the Halloween party, he'd never left his cabin. Tim told me he was worried people would harass him if they knew he was a professor specializing in the Romantic poets." She paused. "I suppose I would have, but only in the most civilized way."

"He seems to have an exaggerated idea of the rock-star appeal of an English professor, Miss Miller, but his background doesn't raise any red flags."

"He's from Montreal. Gerald was from Montreal."

"Actually, he's from Ottawa. He commutes to Concordia. Except this year. This year he's on sabbatical. Unless we're thinking disgruntled student, there doesn't seem to be any reason anyone would want to kill him."

"He seems nervous."

"I'm not surprised, Miss Miller. He came here because he was having trouble getting started on his book. He probably expected peace and quiet, not double homicide." He shrugged. "Sorry, Miss Miller."

She eyed him gravely. "Detective Brisbois, after all we've been through, and you're unwilling to entertain my theories."

"Sorry."

She hopped off the desk. "I'll keep you apprised."

"I appreciate that, Miss Miller."

Creighton shook his head after Miss Miller and Mr. Simpson left. "Last night, she thought someone was setting off firecrackers. Now she thinks it was an assassination." He grinned. "Of course, she was preoccupied last night."

Brisbois picked up his notebook and leafed through it. "Interview with Miss Miller last night. Detective Brisbois: 'What did you think when you heard the shots, Miss Miller?' Miss Miller: 'I thought someone was setting off firecrackers.' Detective Brisbois: 'At midnight?' Miss Miller: 'Please, Detective, we're talking about the Pleasant.'"

He smiled. "She's got something there."

Miss Miller led Simpson up the stairs.

Simpson cleared his throat. "Elizabeth, it seems your theories may be unfounded."

She looked at him over her glasses. "Nonsense, Edward, I find Mr. Harvey's behaviour most suspicious."

"But you must admit, Detective Brisbois' opinions have merit. Mr. Frasor's death may have been nothing more than a tragic accident."

She tapped him on the shoulder. "Edward, I have a plan."

The boss's voice was steely. "I guess you guys screwed up."

Serge composed himself before responding. "Right place, wrong guy. We got bad information."

"The guy's still on site?"

"Yeah. In a different cottage. Turns out he got moved."

"What do the cops know?"

"They don't know squat."

"You know what you've got to do."

"We'll get it done."

"Good. And don't leave a trail." There was a pause. "Figure it out and get back to me. Tout de suite."

Serge winced as the receiver slammed in his ear.

Chapter Sixteen

Tiffany tapped on the door of the High Birches. Adolph opened it a crack, then stepped back when he recognized her.

"I've brought your lunch. An apple, a sandwich, and Mrs. Rudley insisted I bring you a sample of chocolate layer cake and some of Gregoire's thumbprint cookies."

"That's very considerate of Mrs. Rudley."

"Is there anything I can bring you to read?"

"No, I have plenty."

"Please let me know if you need anything."

Adolph took the tray and closed the door. He carried the tray to the table and removed the cover. The salmon sandwich on homemade cracked-wheat bread looked delicious, nicely presented on a floral china plate, cut into quarters, with a dill pickle and a garnish of carrot curls and shredded red cabbage on a bed of baby spinach. They were good here, he thought, going out of their way to dress up his simple requests. Perfect presentation. The apple was polished, its stem removed, and set on a separate plate with a cheese sampler. He took a bite of cheddar and swallowed painfully. He checked the tray. No milk.

As he turned to reach for the telephone, he noted a shadow pass the window. He froze. He had forgotten to lock the door. He got up, stumbled across the room, and fumbled for the lock.

The door slammed into him. A heavyset man shoved him backwards onto the bed. A second man entered, closing the door behind him. The chunky man pinned his upper arms. The other knelt beside him.

"Now, you're going to come with us and you're going to be quiet and you're going to pretend you're enjoying a nice stroll up into the woods. Do anything stupid and we'll waste you and anybody else within shouting distance. Understand?"

Adolph choked on his own saliva. He understood perfectly.

"Edward, we'll take a turn down the lake, then come back up."

Edward rested the paddle across his knees. "Elizabeth, we've been scrutinizing Mr. Harvey for three days and so far the most incriminating thing we've witnessed is him hanging a dishtowel on the clothesline."

"Paddle in the water, Edward."

Tiffany rushed up to the desk where Margaret and Rudley were huddled over the reservation book. "Where is Detective Brisbois?"

Rudley turned a page. "I believe he's out on the porch, contemplating his navel."

Tiffany ran to the door and flung it open. "Detective Brisbois?" She ran back into the lobby, distracted.

Brisbois followed her inside. "What's the matter?"

She paused to catch her breath. "Professor Wyler. He's missing."

"Missing?"

"I took his lunch down earlier, then went on to the Elm Pavilion. When I returned to the kitchen, I noticed a glass of milk on the counter. Gregoire must have forgotten to put it on Professor Wyler's tray. I poured a fresh glass. When I got to the High Birches, he was gone."

Creighton had entered the lobby and stood leaning against the door frame.

"When did you see him last?" Brisbois asked.

"Half an hour ago."

Brisbois turned to the Rudleys. "Have you heard anything from him?"

They shook their heads.

"Not since he called in his lunch order, Detective," Margaret said.

Brisbois put an arm around Tiffany and steered her toward a chair. "He called up for his lunch. You delivered it. Half an hour later, he's missing. Maybe he went for a walk."

Tiffany shook her head. "His lunch was barely touched. He had taken a bite of cheese. The door was ajar."

Margaret frowned. "I don't think he would have gone for a walk, Detective. He hasn't been on the grounds since he arrived. He hasn't come down for a single meal. The Halloween party was his only outing. He might just as well have checked into a hotel in downtown Toronto."

"Do you think he might have decided to walk away without paying his bill?"

Margaret put a hand to her mouth. "That couldn't be. A professor of the Romantic poets?"

Rudley sniffed. "I, for one, Margaret, have always been suspicious of grown men who get misty-eyed over daffodils."

"Lloyd's been out and around," Brisbois said. "Maybe he's seen him."

Rudley turned and bellowed, "Lloyd."

Lloyd came down the hall from the kitchen. "You were wanting me?"

"Yes. The police want to talk to you."

"Have you seen Professor Wyler today?" Brisbois asked.

"Nope."

"I'm sure he didn't run off without paying," Rudley said. "We've never had a guest leave without paying."

"Except Katherine Hepburn," said Lloyd.

Rudley shook his head. "Who could have imagined Katherine Hepburn would leave without paying her bill?"

Brisbois raised his brows. "You had Katherine Hepburn as a guest?"

"As it turned out, her real name was Dianne Thumboldt," Margaret said. "But she looked ever so like Katherine Hepburn. Straight out of *The Philadelphia Story*."

"I thought she looked more like Katherine Hepburn in *Bringing up Baby*."

"Or even in *Morning Glory*," said Lloyd.

Rudley gazed dreamily across the lobby. "Wonderful actress. Real class."

Brisbois cleared his throat. "We were talking about Professor Wyler."

Rudley looked injured. "Well, I don't know how much more I can tell you. If he's gone, he's gone."

Margaret fluttered her hands, distressed. "Detective, something must have happened to him. I can't see him wandering off. As I've said, he's been here almost three weeks and he's not put a toe outside his cottage, except for the party."

"Didn't that strike you as odd?"

"Out of the ordinary, perhaps, but not odd. Every now and then we get some poor soul who needs to get away for a rest." She took Rudley's arm. "Remember Mr. Franklin?"

Rudley glowered.

"Uncomfortable subject, Rudley?"

"We found out later he had come here intending to commit suicide," Margaret went on. "Instead, he developed a crush on Tiffany."

Brisbois smiled. "For once, you have a good story."

"And then he went back to Toronto and got hit by a bus," said Lloyd.

"The point is," said Rudley, "sometimes people come here for reasons other than fishing and society. One man came here hoping to cure his insomnia. Slept like a log his entire stay. Said the frogs' chorus was like a Brahms lullaby."

"They do outdo themselves," said Margaret.

Brisbois looked at Creighton out of the corner of his eye. "We'll be back. He tipped his hat to Margaret and headed for the door.

Creighton stopped a few steps back as Brisbois paused to lean over the railing and stare out over the lake. Finally he launched himself off the railing and headed down the steps and out onto the lawn. Creighton caught up to him halfway to the dock.

"I think the folks have finally lost it," said Creighton.

Brisbois lit a cigarette. "I can't say I blame them." He took a long drag. "We'll give the professor another hour."

"Chances are he just went for a walk."

"I don't know. Maybe Miss Miller was right. Maybe somebody was out to get the professor and they shot Frasor by mistake."

"Or the whole thing could just have been a Halloween prank that went sour."

"Or a hit man who wanted to make the killing look random."

Creighton considered this. "The professor was pretty shaken up. Maybe he just decided to get to hell out of here."

"Could be." Brisbois pushed back his hat. "Look, why don't you call the university? See if anybody there's heard from him."

Serge prodded Adolph through the woods to an outboard camouflaged by a sweep of aspen. "Now, you're going to sit nice and quiet and act as if you're having a good time. We're just three guys out for a ride up the lake."

Adolph stumbled over the seat. "I don't know anything."

"You can tell us all that later. Right now, we're going to get out of here before they miss you too much." He gave Adolph a sharp nudge in the back. "If they miss you at all."

Simpson cleared his throat. "Elizabeth, I'm feeling rather peckish. We've been paddling up and down the lake since breakfast. Let's say we return to the inn for lunch."

"Just a moment. There's a boat headed for Harvey's dock." She picked up her binoculars and gasped. "Edward!"

"Yes?"

"Three men." She turned to him, triumphant. "One of them is Professor Wyler."

He took the binoculars. "I believe you're right, Elizabeth."

"Why would Professor Wyler be headed for Mr. Harvey's with two strange men?"

"They look rather ordinary to me."

She took the binoculars back. "It seems suspicious."

"Probably not as suspicious as us lurking about watching him hang his laundry."

"Paddle, Edward."

After cruising along the shore for fifteen minutes, Mitch manoeuvred the outboard into the boathouse at Harvey's cottage, got out, and tied up. Serge shoved Adolph onto the platform, where he landed in a heap against a support beam.

Serge reached down and hauled him up. "We're going up to the cottage. Don't try anything funny."

They walked single file to the cottage, Adolph sandwiched between them.

*

Tears streamed down Adolph's face. "I've told you, I don't know anything."

"We think you do."

"I don't know where he worked or who he worked for."

Serge tightened his grip on Adolph's collar, while Mitch stod guard over Harvey. "You were his boyfriend and he didn't tell you anything?"

"He wasn't my boyfriend."

"Okay, so he was your friend. Friends tell friends things."

"All I know is he made some films."

"I don't believe you."

Adolph tried to take a deep breath, but choked. "Okay, I know he heard something, but I don't know what it was."

Serge turned away, then turned back and smiled. "Even if I did believe you, I can't let you go. You know that."

Adolph closed his eyes.

Serge smiled. "You two guys are going to have an accident. You were going for a nice ride up the lake. Your boat blows up. End of story."

"You can't do that," Harvey stuttered. "You barged into my house…"

Waving him off, Serge wandered over to the window and peered through the slit between the curtains. "Who are those people out there?"

Harvey stuttered. "What people?"

"Those people in the canoe." He grabbed Harvey and pulled him toward the window. "Those people."

Harvey blinked. "They're guests from the inn across the lake."

"What are they doing here?"

"I don't know."

Serge stepped back from the window, pushing Harvey ahead of him. "You keep things under control," he told Mitch. "I'm going out to see what they want."

*

Simpson dipped his paddle into the water. "I think we should go now, Elizabeth."

"Just a minute," she said. "I want to get a better look at that outboard."

She put her paddle in the water just as Serge stepped out from behind the shrubs.

"Can I help you?"

She smiled. "We were just leaving."

He levelled the rifle. "I don't think that would be polite." He beckoned them ashore.

Simpson started to paddle in. Miss Miller stopped him with a hand to his wrist. "We can wade in from here, Edward. It's not that deep."

He gave a quick nod.

Serge grinned. "Come on, let's join the fun."

*

Brisbois was pacing up and down the veranda when Creighton bounded out.

"You're going to like this, boss."

"Something tells me I won't."

"I got on the phone to the university. The woman I talked to, Pauline Talbot, told me that Professor Wyler checked in with her this morning."

"Yeah?"

"He said he just got home from northern Quebec yesterday. He checked in for his messages. She told him the police had been asking about him. She said he seemed quite puzzled. So I asked if maybe there was another Wyler on sabbatical from the English department. She says there's just one of them."

"Go on."

"I described our Professor Wyler and she said he sounded a lot like Adolph Green, the professor's admin assistant who, by coincidence, is on leave to attend to a family emergency."

"Okay."

"She's not prepared to give out any more information without checking our credentials. I asked her to send a photo to our friends in the Montreal constabulary. They'll fax it to us."

"How long?"

"Within the hour."

*

Serge held the rifle as Mitch prepared to bind the group with duct tape.

"You won't get away with this," Miss Miller said.

Serge shrugged. "I think we will."

"They'll miss us at the inn. They'll call the police."

"Do her first," Serge told Mitch. "I'm tired of listening to her. You," he said as Simpson took a step forward. "One more move and I'll plug her where she stands. Do him next," he instructed Mitch. "The other two don't seem as frisky."

Serge watched as Mitch secured the captives' arms and slapped duct tape over their mouths. "Okay, let's walk them down to the boat. We'll do their legs once we get them in." He looked toward the door. "I'll go out and take a look around first."

He returned a few minutes later. "It's clear."

*

Brisbois contacted headquarters then returned to join Creighton on the veranda. He lit a cigarette while he considered his next move. His gaze fixed on an outboard cutting toward the shore, towing a canoe. The navigator cut the engine and drifted toward the dock. The man called to Lloyd, who was turning over a flowerbed at the bottom of the yard.

"That canoe looks like one of the Pleasant's," Creighton observed.

Brisbois levered himself off the railing. "Come on. Maybe someone's in trouble."

"Found it riding against the reed bank on the north side," the man explained when they arrived at the dock. "I knew it was the Pleasant's logo. I looked around. Didn't see anybody in the water. I thought I'd bring it in and see if anybody knew about it. Maybe one just got away, although I don't know how it would end up over there."

Brisbois introduced himself and Creighton.

"Bob Smith," the man said.

"Exactly where did you find the boat, Mr. Smith?"

"Near the Harvey place."

Brisbois jotted down the man's name.

"That's the one Miss Miller and Mr. Simpson took out," said Lloyd.

"You're sure?"

"Only one out."

"Did they say where they were going?"

Lloyd grinned. "Miss Miller said they were going on an investigation."

Brisbois turned to Creighton. "That sounds familiar." He turned his attention back to Lloyd. "Can you find us an outboard?"

"One with lights?"

"That would be nice."

"And a big motor?"

"Sure."

Lloyd trotted off to the boathouse and returned idling a motorboat up to the dock. "Now, you've got to be real careful getting in on account your shoes are slippery."

"We'll be careful."

"And there's an oar under there for when you get stuck in the weeds."

"We won't get stuck."

"And the lifejackets are under the seats." He grinned. "You get fined if you get caught not wearing them."

"Put on your lifejacket, Creighton."

"And there's a tow rope for when you need to get towed."

"We won't need to get towed."

"And if you get stalled, you turn it like so."

"Yes, Lloyd."

"And you turn it this way and that to go where you're going."

"Okay."

"And there's a compass in that little pocket there for when you get lost."

"Lloyd?"

"Yes'm?"

"Get out of the boat."

"Yes'm."

"Go up to the inn and tell Rudley we've gone out to Harvey's place because Mr. Smith here found one of his canoes in the reeds over there."

"Do you want him to call the police?"

Brisbois held up his cellphone. "We'll do that if we need to."

Creighton got into the boat and positioned himself at the stern. "You're driving?"

"I'm a natural."

"All right." Brisbois sat down. "We'll head over, check with Harvey. There's no point in bringing the patrol boat out if they just stopped by for a chat and forgot to pull the canoe up."

Creighton accelerated away from the dock. "You realize we don't have our Kevlars."

Brisbois ducked to light a cigarette. "We're just taking a run across the lake. What do we need our Kevlars for?'"

"Oh, I thought they might come in handy if someone starts shooting at us with a high-powered rifle."

"I don't think that's likely to happen."

Creighton turned left. "Yeah, hardly seems likely. After all, we've just had some crazy knocking off one of the guests and we're out here in a boat in suits and ties with our gun holsters. We might as well have POLICE stamped on our foreheads. Not as if we're a tempting target."

Brisbois shrugged. "We'll be watchful. If we see something we don't like, we'll call in reinforcements."

Creighton steered clear of the shoal markers. "You know, Brisbois, my last partner wouldn't put his foot out the door without posting his destination with coordinates. If there was a chance of running into a six-year-old with a popgun, the Kevlars went on. He called in backup if his horoscope didn't read right."

Brisbois let the breeze shear the ash from his cigarette. "What's your point?"

Creighton gave him a long look, then sighed. "That life with him was pretty boring. That's what I wanted to say."

Serge and Mitch marched the group to Harvey's boat, a twenty-five-foot cabin cruiser, pushed them into the hold, and tied their legs. They locked the door and went topside.

Serge checked the gas gauge. "We'll go down the lake to that bunch of islands, whack them on the head, untie them, sprinkle lots of gasoline around. They went out for a cruise and had a tragic accident. We'll be back in Montreal by the time anyone figures out who they are." He gestured to the smaller outboard alongside Harvey's cabin cruiser. "Tie that good. Otherwise, we'll have a nice cold swim."

Mitch examined the control console. "Do you know how to drive this thing?"

Serge gave him a long stare. "As long as we take it easy, we'll be fine."

"I don't know why we couldn't have gone out in the middle of the night and slit a few throats."

"Because the boss wants to make it all look like an accident."

"I'd rather do somebody in the business any day. Nobody wants to make a federal case out of it."

Serge smirked. "Think of it as expanding your horizons."

"I think it just makes more chances for a foul-up."

"Maybe. But he pays the bill so he calls the shots."

"Why do we have to whack them? Why can't we just leave them tied up?"

Serge slapped the wheel. "Now would that be nice? Burning them alive while they're still conscious? Besides, it's not going to look much like an accident if they're tied up."

"They look like a bunch of dumb fucks to me. Ain't worth the price of the gasoline."

"Yeah, they don't look like much." Serge idled the boat out of the cove. "Grab a beer or whatever he's got in that cooler and act natural. We're just two guys having a nice run down the lake."

"Edward." Miss Miller rolled to her side and came nose to nose with Simpson.

"Urgh, urgh, urgh."

She smiled.

His eyebrows knit in a question.

"He didn't make the tape tight enough. I worked it off with my tongue. If you hold still, I'll get yours." She wriggled around, turned her head, caught the edge of the tape in her teeth and pulled.

Simpson's eyes budged. "Hm, hm, hm."

"Be brave, Edward." She worked the tape loose.

He took a deep breath and exhaled slowly. "Now what, Elizabeth?" He glanced at Harvey and Adolph. Their eyes were wide and imploring. "I think you'll have to wait until we get our hands free." He turned to Miss Miller. "How do you propose we do that?"

"There must be something around here." She rocked across to the cabinets and rolled to her knees. "Help me, Edward."

"As you wish." He rolled over, got his shoulder under her rear end, and hoisted her upright.

She opened a drawer with her teeth. Tea towels. Tried the next. Knick-knacks. The third yielded plastic bags. She paused and looked around. "Aha." She hopped over, ducked her head into the sink, and, after a few tries, came up with a knife in her teeth. "Now, Edward," she said around the knife, "you will have to stand up and let me place the knife in your hands. I will back up and you will work the knife against the tape."

Harvey stared in horror. Adolph winced.

Edward took a deep breath. "Don't worry, gentlemen. She does this sort of thing all the time."

*

Mitch put a hand over his eyes and searched the shoreline. "How far do we have to go before we dump this crowd?"

"Not until we get into the islands."

"Why can't we dump them now?"

Serge stared straight ahead. "You want to dump them in front of somebody's cottage? Where somebody can see us from the road? You want to get knee-capped?"

Mitch swallowed hard. "When do we get there?"

"Half an hour."

"Can't we open this thing up?"

Serge gave him an oblique look. "Sure, if you want me to run this damn thing up on the rocks, I can open it up full throttle."

Mitch slumped into the jump seat.

*

"Be careful, Edward, I think you're perilously close to my radial artery."

"I'm sorry, Elizabeth. It's difficult to avoid these things when you're cutting backwards with your hands bound together."

"Stop." Miss Miller thought for a moment. "Keep your hands still and I'll move up and down against the blade."

"Roger that."

*

Brisbois pointed to the reed bank. "Pull in around there. That's where the guy found the canoe."

Creighton killed the motor, picked up the paddle, and moved in close to the bank. Brisbois scanned the shore, brow furrowed.

"I don't think anything happened," Creighton said. "Miss Miller is a strong swimmer. Besides, the canoe probably just drifted away. Maybe she didn't pull it up far enough."

"That's not like Miss Miller."

"Maybe she left Simpson to pull it up."

"That's definitely not like Miss Miller."

Creighton poked along the shoreline. As they pulled into the dock at Harvey's cottage, a red-winged blackbird erupted from the reeds. Brisbois started, lost his balance, and fell hard against the side of the dock.

Creighton reached to haul him up. "Are you all right?"

"I'm fine." Brisbois patted his pockets and searched the bottom of the boat. "Damn."

"What's the matter?"

"My cellphone. It must have slipped out of my pocket when I fell."

Creighton glanced around the dock. "I hate to tell you but it's probably in the drink."

Brisbois straightened his jacket. "You've got yours, haven't you?"

Creighton gave him a sheepish smile. "It's back at the inn. I forgot to take it out of the charger."

Brisbois shrugged. "We can use Harvey's phone if we need to." He started up the path toward the cottage.

Creighton did a quick reconnoitre, then followed.

Brisbois thumped on the door, then glanced around as he waited for an answer. "Nice place. Lots of privacy."

"Maybe he's up to something that needs a lot of privacy."

"Hard to believe, given his background." Brisbois frowned and thumped the door again. "Not that that means anything. He wouldn't be the first upstanding citizen to turn to the dark side."

Creighton glanced back at the dock. "I wonder where he keeps his big boat."

"Probably in the big boathouse." Brisbois gestured toward the tan building with the weathervane." He leaned to one side to look through the window. "Doesn't look as if anybody's home." He tried the latch. The door opened. "Let's take a look. Just in case he's in trouble." He stepped inside, looked around, then held up a hand. "Don't touch anything. Something's not right."

*

"Edward, I'm free." Miss Miller turned. "Give me the knife." She cut the tape from her legs, then turned to free Simpson.

Adolph and Harvey looked at her. Simpson massaged his wrists. Miss Miller freed Adolph.

"Miss Miller," Harvey prompted.

Miss Miller gave him a calculating look. "First, I need some answers."

Harvey nodded.

"Who are those men?"

"I have no idea."

"Why did they come here?"

"I don't know, Miss Miller. I answered the door. They were on the porch with the professor."

Miss Miller turned to Adolph. "Professor?"

Adolph gulped. "I don't know who they are."

"What were you doing with them?"

"They're trying to kill me. They…" He stopped, teeth chattering.

"I think they're trying to kill all of us, Elizabeth," said Simpson.

She leaned to him, whispered, "Edward, don't take your eyes off them for a second."

*

Rudley leaned over the desk. "None of this makes any sense to me, Margaret."

"I don't know if it's supposed to, Rudley."

"Professor Wyler runs off without paying his bill. Miss Miller and Mr. Simpson go off in the canoe. The canoe is found floating up the lake. Brisbois and Creighton go off in a motorboat. We don't know what they have in mind."

"They're trying to solve the case, dear."

"I suppose."

"Poor Gerald."

"I beg your pardon?"

"Gerald. Being murdered. It sounds as if he hadn't been doing that well before either."

He nodded.

"And poor Mr. Frasor. Minding his own business. You never know."

"Tragic, Margaret." Rudley peeled himself off the desk, went into the cupboard, brought out a box of receipts, and began to sort through them. "You know, Margaret, it would do my heart good if these people would find somewhere else to commit their murders."

"I doubt if our situation is that unusual, Rudley. Statistically speaking. Other places must have their share."

"Ott at the Bridal Path would have a heart attack if someone sprained an ankle on his property. McFarlane won't let anyone take a boat out without signing a release." Rudley tore a receipt out, crumpled it, and threw it toward the wastepaper basket. "The Pleasant has become the murder capital of North America."

"Perhaps it's what they call the cluster phenomenon."

Lloyd came into the lobby, holding a hammer. He stopped in front of the desk.

"Are you here to do us in or do you have work to do?"

"Gregoire needs a board tapped down in the pantry."

"Is Brisbois back yet?"

"Nope."

"It seems strange that Miss Miller and Simpson would lose a canoe."

"She must have let Simpson pull it up."

Margaret frowned. "We should worry about Detective Brisbois being out too late. It'll be dark soon and you know how he is around boats."

"Like a pig on ice." Rudley chuckled. "As I recall, the last time he brought his wife here, he dumped her into the lake trying to tie the boat up."

"Maybe we should call the police. You know what trouble he can get into."

Rudley stuffed a handful of receipts into the box and coaxed it shut. "I know he's come close to getting his head blown off, Margaret, but that was just once. He should have learned to have his wits about him by now."

Margaret rescued the receipt box and smoothed out the papers. "If he's not back by dusk, I'm calling the police."

*

"What now, Elizabeth?"

They huddled in the hold, Harvey's face blotched from the tape, Adolph's moustache considerably thinned.

She proceeded with confidence. "Our best strategy is to wait for an opportunity to take them by surprise. They have some evil-looking rifles and I doubt if they would hesitate to use them."

"I'm quite sure of that," said Harvey. His eyes looked owlish in the dim light.

Adolph shuddered.

"Cold, son?"

Adolph shook his head.

"Good imagination?"

Adolph turned his face away from Harvey.

"If you don't mind," said Simpson, "it's cruel to pester Professor Wyler."

"It seems he's the reason we're in this mess."

"We can sort that out later," Simpson said.

"If we hear one of them coming," Miss Miller said, "we'll stand against the wall behind the door and give him a good whack on the head as he enters." She hefted a jam jar. "Once we get one of them out of the way, we'll have the advantage."

"What if they both come down with guns blazing?"

"Then I shall throw myself upon them while you cower in the corner, Mr. Harvey."

Simpson spoke up. "I think Elizabeth's plan is our best hope, Mr. Harvey."

Harvey crossed himself.

Chapter Seventeen

Brisbois walked out onto the porch, hands stuffed into his pockets. "Something happened in there. Chair knocked over, broken vase, flowers, water on the floor. I can't see someone going off and leaving a mess like that."

"Didn't notice a cat around," said Creighton.

"Let's check out the boathouse."

"Would be nice if he had a phone," Creighton added.

"Now we know why Harvey dropped by the Pleasant instead of phoning."

They climbed up a short rise, passing under a stand of weeping willows.

"Beautiful place," Brisbois remarked.

"Inboard's gone," Creighton said when they arrived at the boathouse.

"Try this: Miss Miller and Simpson go off on a canoe trip. They stop at Mr. Harvey's. He invites them to go for a ride in his boat." Brisbois tipped his hat forward and massaged the back of his neck. "Except the house was a mess."

"Try this, then," Creighton responded. "Somebody bumps into the table, knocks over the vase, and grabs the chair for support. It falls over. Harvey planned to take his guests for a boat ride. He decides to clean up the mess when he gets back. It's getting late. He wants to take advantage of the daylight."

Brisbois frowned. "How long would it take to pick up a vase, straighten a chair, and clean up a small puddle of water?"

Creighton looked across the lake. "Boss, I think we should go back to the Pleasant and phone in, get the patrol boat to take a look around."

Brisbois nodded. "Let's take a run up the other way, take a quick look around, then we'll go back to the inn."

Margaret's hand hovered over the telephone. "Rudley, I'm calling the police."

"Give them another few minutes, Margaret."

Margaret glanced at the clock. "The hour's up. We agreed we'd call."

"Very well. But you realize we'll look like complete fools when they arrive back safe and sound."

"Better safe than sorry."

Serge checked his watch. "We should be in the middle of the islands in ten minutes."

"Should I go down now?"

Serge's gaze swept the horizon. He stiffened. "Stay cool. There's an outboard on our tail."

Brisbois leaned forward. "That's Harvey's boat."

"I see it."

"Can you go any faster?"

"Opening her up."

"Pull alongside."

Serge jerked his head toward a pair of binoculars suspended from a hook under the control console. "See what's up with that boat."

Mitch took the binoculars and squinted into them. "A couple of guys in suits and ties. You've got to be kidding."

Serge grabbed the binoculars and took a look. He slammed them into Mitch's chest. "Cops."

"Maybe we can outrun them."

Serge licked his lips. "No. We'll let them come alongside. We're just two guys out for a boat trip. If we don't like the way things are going" — he nodded toward the rifles — "blow them out of the water."

"They're slowing down," Creighton said.

"I guess they want to talk to us."

Miss Miller crept to the door. "They're stopping."

Edward touched her shoulder. "That might not be good news, Elizabeth."

Adolph blanched.

Brisbois stood up and waved his arms. "Gentlemen." His eyes swept the cabin cruiser.

Serge turned to Mitch and nodded. Creighton's hand moved toward his holster. Too late. Bullets danced in the water, ripping through the bow of the outboard. Brisbois pitched into the water. Creighton ducked behind the boat as it capsized.

Brisbois surfaced beside him. A bullet splintered wood inches above their heads.

"Duck." Creighton dove, dragging Brisbois with him.

Serge turned to Mitch. "Lousy shooting."

"The boat was moving around." Mitch stared at the water. "I think I got them."

"There's probably more coming." Serge wavered, hand on the wheel. "Okay, set the damn thing on fire and get ready to ditch." He grabbed a can of gasoline. "If you forgot to tie that outboard down, now's the time to tell me."

Simpson's nose wrinkled. "I smell gasoline. I believe they're about to scuttle the boat." He gave Miss Miller an aggrieved look. "What now, Elizabeth?"

Brisbois and Creighton surfaced against the side of the inboard. Creighton grabbed Brisbois' hand and plastered it to a bumper. "Hang onto this."

They heard a splash.

"Either that's a big fish or somebody's going for a swim," Creighton whispered.

They heard a second splash. An outboard motor spluttered, then caught.

"We've got to get onto that boat." Brisbois grabbed the rope attached to the bumper and hauled himself up the side.

Creighton followed.

"We're on fire," Brisbois gasped. He struggled over the rail.

The deck was a wall of flames. Brisbois recoiled against the railing. He heard pounding from the hold. He ran to the door and kicked hard. The door broke open. Miss Miller, Simpson, Harvey, and Adolph tumbled out.

Creighton grabbed the fire extinguisher. "Everybody go starboard and bail," he shouted.

Adolph hovered at the railing. "I can't swim."

Creighton snatched a cushion from a deck chair and threw it at him. "Take this and get the hell out of here." He fought the fire until everyone had jumped, then flung the exhausted extinguisher at the flames, and dove over the railing.

They swam away from the boat, Miss Miller hauling Adolph in her wake. Harvey led the way with surprising grace and strength. Creighton thrust the cushion toward Brisbois. "I think you'd better have this."

"It looks like a long way to shore."

Creighton threw his head back to clear the hair from his eyes. "Just stick with me."

Brisbois thought he'd rather stick with Miss Miller, but she had Adolph to contend with.

An explosion ripped the air as the fire hit the gas tank.

"That should bring someone," Creighton said.

"Hope so," Brisbois gasped. "This water's damned cold."

Creighton scanned the horizon. "I'll be…"

Two outboards were making their way toward them.

"I think we're saved," said Creighton.

"Margaret phoned the police," Rudley said. "But she didn't think they were taking her seriously."

"They didn't express sufficient urgency to suit me," Margaret said. "So we decided to take a look for ourselves."

"Then we got partway out and heard a big bang and saw things flying through the air," Lloyd added. "And Mr. Rudley said, 'There they go.'"

Simpson flinched.

"Your timing was perfect," said Miss Miller. "We would have had trouble, keeping everyone together in the dark."

Rudley folded his arms. "All in a day's work."

Creighton came into the lobby, looking svelte in a pair of Tim's jeans and a white shirt. He laughed when he saw Brisbois in one of Mr. Sawchuck's golf shirts and shorts. "Cute."

Brisbois gave him a stern look. "What's the word?"

"Our guys found the getaway boat, partially submerged, a half-mile up from where the boat exploded. They're checking it out."

"Any sign of our pirates?"

"Nothing. They searched the shoreline where the boat was scuttled. No footprints. There's a big sheet of rock up there, where they might have come ashore. Or maybe they did us a favour and drowned."

"They were wearing lifejackets." Brisbois sighed. "Well, we've got a pretty good description."

Creighton flipped open his notebook. "The one guy, slightly above average height. Mesomorphic build." He winked. "That was from Miss Miller."

She tilted her head and smiled.

"The other one, maybe five-seven. Chunky. Black ball caps, mirrored sunglasses. Jeans. Windbreakers. One black, one navy. Maple Leaf logos on the caps and jackets. No visible scars or tattoos.

One was wearing black leather gloves. The other one, driving gloves. Grey with black palms. Moustaches. No beards."

"With that description you could arrest Reg and his son from the marina."

"Mind your manners, Rudley." Margaret paused. "They wouldn't have got away with this in the summer. The cottagers would have noticed right away when the boat blew up and would have been waiting at the shore."

"I noticed it right away," Simpson murmured.

"Did they say how Harvey's doing?" Brisbois asked.

"They don't think he had a heart attack or anything," Creighton reported. "They think he may have pulled some rib muscles hauling his great bulk through the cold water. They're keeping him in hospital overnight for observation."

"It's a shame you had to take Adolph in," Margaret said. "He must be terrified."

Brisbois nodded. "At least he's alive." So far, Adolph hadn't been able to give them much information. He stuck to his alias until confronted with the picture the university had provided along with the news of the real Professor Wyler's return. He didn't know who the gunmen were. He knew only that Gerald had been making questionable films and had witnessed a drug deal going down. He understood the films were pornographic, possibly involving underage actors. He had no idea of the location of the studio or the name of the man Gerald referred to only as "the director." They were frightened; they had run. Brisbois didn't blame them.

He sat back and detached himself from the conversation, which had turned to anecdotes of Adolph's stay at the Pleasant.

Gerald had got himself killed and had put his friend in jeopardy by consorting with the seamy side. And for what? It couldn't have been the money. He probably didn't get more than a couple of hundred per performance. Blinded by the dream of a legitimate film career? Maybe that was all there was to it.

He was disposed to believe Adolph was an innocent bystander. Professor Wyler had vouched for him, describing him as conscientious, good-hearted, and timid. Gerald had taken advantage of Adolph, the same as he had taken advantage of Gregoire. He was a user, pure and simple. Still, he didn't deserve to be murdered.

"Phone for you."

"Eh?"

Rudley hit him in the elbow with the receiver. "The phone. It's for you."

"Oh." Brisbois took the phone. "Yes, it probably would have," he said, frowning into the receiver. "It turned out all right in the end." He rolled his eyes. "Inspector, did you call me for any reason other than to gloat about me losing my cellphone?" He nodded. "And having the boat blow up?" He listened, lifted his eyebrows and took out his notebook. "You don't say? Yeah? Right away."

He hung up, put a hand on Creighton's shoulder, and steered him out onto the veranda. "The inspector just took a call from one of the patrol cars. He got the call because, as he pointed out, my phone wasn't working. Apparently, the officer never thought to call me here. They found a few things in a garbage can behind a place up the lake."

"Are you going to tell me what and where?"

"Baseball caps and windbreakers. On the property of one James Devlin."

"I guess we're headed that way. By car, I hope."

"Yeah, yeah." Brisbois stepped into the doorway. "Folks, we're leaving. Dispatch will know where to reach us if you need us."

"We won't need you," Rudley hollered.

"I don't think he enjoys our company," said Creighton.

They walked down to the car.

Creighton opened the driver's door. "Have they talked to Devlin?"

"He isn't home. There's a search warrant coming."

Brisbois was quiet as the car swung out of the driveway and along the shore road. The air smelled like fermenting apples and the dried leaves that swirled in the fickle breeze. A few leaves clung to the branches. Not enough to hide the full moon. What was it about this place that attracted murder?

"They must think the law's pretty stupid out here," he remarked.

Creighton was concentrating on the ditch where an occasional pair of bright animal eyes glinted in the tall grass. "Come again?"

"If Devlin were involved, why would he let his flunkies dump their stuff in his garbage can?"

"Because they think we're stupid." Creighton raised an index finger. "Or they're stupid. Or they were in a big hurry. Or they just threw the stuff in the first convenient trash can. Or they're trying to set Devlin up."

Brisbois pushed his body back against the seat, seeking relief for his aching back. Jesus, he wasn't used to getting blown into the water, fumbling around on a burning boat, and swimming for his life on the same afternoon. "I'm going to get my back checked out once this case is over."

"We might want to get our heads checked out, too."

"What do we know about Devlin?"

Creighton shrugged. "Handsome young guy from Toronto. Studied at Sheridan College. Ran a small upscale restaurant in Cabbagetown. Moved out here and opened a bed and breakfast when he got tired of the downtown scene. Parents still living in Maple. Brother in Saskatoon. Sister in Welland. Never married."

"His place has been shut down for the last couple of weeks."

"Yeah. Kitchen renovations. According to Rudley, he's off on some artistic jaunt this weekend. Portland. He's showing some of his stuff. Then he's got a trip booked to Marrakesh."

"Kind of coincidental."

"Maybe not. If you're going to shut down a B&B, this is a good time to do it. Rudley says business gets pretty heavy once the snow flies. Cross-country skiing, downhill skiing, ice-fishing."

"That I could go for." Brisbois squirmed and adjusted the seat. "According to Margaret, Devlin was supposed to be at the party. He phoned in the morning with his apologies. When we interviewed him, he said he started out for the inn but his motor conked out. He tried to get it going but couldn't. Had to paddle back to his place. He said by the time he got home it was late and he was covered in grease. So he just went to bed. What's to say he didn't run his boat up into the cove near the point, shoot the place up, hop into his boat, and go home?"

Creighton shook his head. "I can't see it."

"What about the lights Watkins saw on the water?"

"He wasn't sure what he saw. He thought it might have been moonlight."

"Rudley doesn't like Devlin much," Brisbois said.

"Rudley doesn't like him because he's a good-looking guy and he's taken a liking to Margaret."

"She's teaching him to paint."

Creighton stole a look at Brisbois. "Almost everybody takes a liking to Margaret."

"Why wouldn't they?"

Creighton smiled. "No reason they wouldn't." When Brisbois didn't respond, he said. "That was good news about Harvey anyway. I think he thought he was a goner when they were loading him into the ambulance."

"Poor devil," Brisbois said. "I think he started to have the chest pains when he finally got it that the boat was gone for good. He started talking about how he and his wife had worked on it for years. It was a pile of junk when they got it. They were planning to retire to a cottage near their home in Michigan."

"Then she died?"

"Then she was killed in a car accident. He was driving. He was exonerated, but her family blamed him. Harassed him so much he left."

"Nice people."

"Yeah." Brisbois took a deep breath, exhaled sharply. "Yeah, he really thought he was going to die. Maybe he wanted the people with him to know his story."

The flashing lights of a cruiser told them they had arrived at Devlin's. Creighton pulled in behind a black and white and got out. Brisbois struggled out after him.

"The Inspector says you found some stuff," Brisbois said by way of greeting.

The officer took a look at Brisbois' outfit, then ducked his head to hide a smirk. "This way." He led him to the back of the house and pointed to the metal garbage can. "Somebody tried to burn the stuff up, but they were dense enough to put the lid on."

Brisbois peeked into the can. "Stuff got singed, then the oxygen gave out." He turned to the officer. "Anything else?"

"No. No sign of the fugitives." He gestured into the woods. "We've got three units looking around up there. So far, nothing. They probably had somebody waiting for them up by the road. They could be anywhere by now."

A cruiser pulled up. A patrolman got out and handed Brisbois a paper. "Here's your search warrant."

Chapter Eighteeen

Brisbois and Creighton dragged themselves into the inn after nine. Margaret was at the desk.

"Detectives, you look worn out."

"It's been that kind of day, Margaret."

"We saved you some roast beef and Gregoire has a wonderful raspberry bombe."

"As long as it doesn't explode." Brisbois reached up to remove his hat, then realized he didn't have one. "Sorry, it's been a long day."

"Go ahead into the dining room. Tim will get you whatever you want."

"Thanks." Brisbois paused. "This workshop Jim Devlin was going to, was it something spontaneous?"

"Oh, no. He registered for the workshop months ago. Signed up for several sessions in watercolours."

"Did he say he'd planned to leave this morning?"

"Yes, there was a watercolorist from New York giving an afternoon session. He was particularly interested in his technique."

"I thought you were giving him lessons."

"I've given him some pointers, but I think it's wise of him to broaden his perspective. Otherwise his stuff would look much like mine."

"That wouldn't be so bad, would it?"

"Thank you, Detective, but let me put it this way — how many Picassos would you want?"

"None would be enough for me. I find watercolours easy on the eye." He paused. "Do you have the phone number for that workshop?"

"I'll get you the brochure." She waved at Tim as he passed the doorway of the dining room. "Tim, would you get something nice for these gentlemen?" She called to Rudley, who had just come across from the kitchen. "Rudley, would you mind the desk? I won't be but a minute."

"Of course, Margaret." Rudley slipped behind the desk. "Brisbois, I hear you're after Devlin now."

Brisbois gave him a bemused smile. "Where did you hear that rumour?"

"Officer Owens dropped by. He admitted, after some casual interrogation, that you were over there ransacking the place."

"Just being thorough." Brisbois gave Rudley a salute and nudged Creighton toward the dining room.

Rudley did a quick shuffle and beat out a tune on the desktop. I knew that young pup Devlin was up to no good, he thought. Imagine, befriending Margaret to get a toehold into the affairs of the inn. To monitor our situation. And everyone chasing after poor old Harvey. Chalk one up for the old guys!

"You seem to have recovered," he said to Miss Miller, who had come down the stairs, followed by Simpson.

"I pride myself on my resilience, Mr. Rudley."

Rudley cast a quizzical glance toward Simpson.

He blushed. "Elizabeth is definitely resilient."

Gregoire came out of the kitchen with a bottle of wine, followed by Tim, rolling covered dishes on a trolley.

"For you, detectives," said Gregoire, "because of your trauma today. A bottle of our finest red. On the house."

"Oh, we couldn't."

"We'll send the bill to your department. Surely you are entitled to a decent meal for practically drowning. You get a meal allowance when you are on location."

"Yes, for Joe's Diner."

"The dinner prices are much lower after ten. Mostly the same as Joe's Diner."

Tim placed the chafing dishes on the sideboard. "Prime rib, salad with a mustard dressing, baked potato, carrots glazed with lemon and a secret ingredient I am not at liberty to divulge. And the coup de grâce, raspberry bombe."

Creighton flicked out his napkin and settled it in his lap. "Dig in, boss, it's on the account."

Brisbois hesitated, then acquiesced. "Sit down for a minute, gentlemen." He pointed to the carafe. "It's the end of the day. Have a cup of coffee."

They sat down. Gregoire removed his cap.

"What do you know about Jim Devlin?"

Gregoire sniffed. "He's a glamour puss. He runs a guest house with Laura Ashley as his inspiration and thinks he has a much better kitchen than he does."

"I hear it's being renovated," said Creighton.

"I'm not talking about the appliances at his disposal. I'm talking about the quality of his menu." He shrugged. "I can cook circles around him on a campfire."

Brisbois took out his notebook. "Apart from the fact that you don't like his décor and think his menu is overrated, what do you think of him?"

"He is one of these good-looking men with air between his ears."

"He's an artist. He must have soul."

Gregoire glowered. "He's an artist because he wants to get in good with Margaret to establish himself in the area for business reasons. After all, everybody loves Mrs. Rudley. A recommendation from her is like gold."

Brisbois looked to Tim. "What do you think?"

"Of course everyone loves Mrs. Rudley. Jim Devlin is very fond of himself, very fond of the reaction he gets from the ladies. Fonder of the reaction than the ladies."

"Are you implying he's gay?"

Tim laughed. "Perish the thought. He's narcissistic. He can't pass a mirror without stopping."

"Criminal?"

"He's too dumb to be criminal."

"Not the sharpest knife in the drawer?"

Gregoire folded his arms. "He is as dull as a bag of hammers, Detective."

Brisbois scribbled a note. "Most of the criminals I've met wouldn't break a hundred on the IQ test."

Tim chuckled. "I think they have what's called peasant cunning. This guy's just a good-looking goof who knows how to dress to bring out the colour in his eyes."

"Maybe it's an act."

"If it is, he should be on Broadway."

Brisbois glanced up. "Miss Miller, Simpson. How are you doing?"

"Exhilarated."

Simpson winced. "I must say, Detective, I shudder to think how close we came to ending up at the bottom of the lake."

Miss Miller took a chair to Brisbois' left. "We would have surfaced eventually, Edward."

Gregoire stood. "Are you ready to have dinner? Perhaps what the detectives are having."

"A slice of that nice roast beef on a bun would hit the spot."

"Coming right up." Tim jumped up and disappeared into the kitchen.

Brisbois leaned over the table as Gregoire and Tim exited the dining room. "Now that you've recovered, Miss Miller, would you clarify for me what you were investigating?"

"Mr. Harvey."

"Because of what he said about the professor?" He shook his head. "I mean, about Adolph?"

"Among other things. Living over there in that secluded cottage. Lurking about here, positioning himself like a large fly on the wall. That strange smile. Those busy eyes."

"I take it you've had him under surveillance."

"You never know what may turn up."

Brisbois picked up a spoon and stirred his coffee. "What turned up was that he was trussed up like a Christmas turkey and tossed into the hold with the rest of you."

"I think that was part of the plan," said Miss Miller.

"So," said Brisbois, tapping the spoon against his cup and replacing it on the saucer, "you thought he was putting on an act. To throw you off balance. To divert suspicion."

"Yes. And who else would have had the opportunity to find out where Adolph was staying?"

Creighton chuckled. "How about every Tom, Dick, and Harry who walks through the door?"

Miss Miller did not chuckle. "Wouldn't you say it's true, Detective, that everyone who deals with the Pleasant has been doing so for years?"

"For the most part."

"So Mr. Harvey and Mr. Devlin are the only regular visitors without a history at the Pleasant, but with ample opportunity."

Brisbois shook his head. "I think your deductions are strongly influenced by your bias, Miss Miller. There are dozens of people in and out of here every day. It wouldn't have been that hard to find out where Adolph was staying. Maybe our kidnappers stopped in for a drink."

She ignored him. "What do you know about Mr. Harvey anyway?"

"He's a retired teacher from Michigan with an impeccable past."

Simpson frowned. "If I may ask, why would someone from Michigan retire to a lake here. Doesn't Michigan have a surplus of lakes?"

"Trust me on this one," said Brisbois. "Mr. Harvey's reasons for coming here were personal, not criminal."

"But what about that boat?" Miss Miller demanded. "On a teacher's salary?"

"He told me it was a wreck when he bought it. He rebuilt it himself."

Miss Miller was not swayed. "I'm sure there's something sinister in his background."

"Not a thing."

"But what about the comment he made about the professor being shot?"

"A reasonable explanation," Brisbois said, "is that he overheard Rudley ask Lloyd to take a meal to the professor at the Oaks. When he heard the person at the Oaks had been shot, he assumed it was the professor. Or Adolph, as it turns out."

Miss Miller looked peeved. "Why would they take Adolph to Harvey's cottage?"

Brisbois paused over a baby carrot. "Maybe because he lives in a secluded location and has a nice big boat."

"How would they know that?"

"Small-town people talk." Creighton scooped up a mound of mashed potatoes and winked at Brisbois. "Or maybe they saw you out there, Miss Miller, and decided to hightail it to the nearest safe harbour."

"Mr. Harvey got the impression they were trying to set things up to look like an accident," Brisbois said. "They wanted a secluded location and they wanted a big boat. He had both."

"Still, it seems suspicious."

Brisbois traced a line along his jaw with his thumb. "You're missing one critical element, Miss Miller."

She raised her brows.

"Motive."

"I don't know that. Yet."

Creighton picked up a roll, severed it neatly with a table knife, and reached for the butter. "And don't forget. They tried to kill him, too."

"There is no honour among thieves," said Miss Miller. "Besides, as we've discussed, that might have been a ruse. They planned to spare him in the end."

Brisbois shook his head. "I'm afraid your imagination has gotten away on you, Miss Miller." He paused as Tim brought out the roast beef sandwiches.

"Anything else for you, Detectives?"

"No, thanks, Tim. Our compliments to the chef." Brisbois turned to Miss Miller. "Enough shop talk. Tell us more about your trip to Outer Mongolia."

Brisbois and Creighton left the inn at eleven, leaving Owens and Semple to patrol the grounds.

"I don't know if Owens is the right guy for this detail," Creighton said. "He'll be so distracted mooning over Tiffany that someone could walk right in and gun the folks down."

Brisbois shrugged. "Or he'll be even more motivated." He paused. "Do you think he has a chance?"

"I don't think he's her type. Christopher Watkins seems to be her type. He doesn't have a lot in common with Owens."

"He's a good kid. She's a nice young woman. She's been going out with guys like Christopher. Nothing's ever come of it. Maybe those guys aren't her type after all. Maybe she just thinks they should be." He paused. "You dated an English major once, didn't you?"

"Yeah."

"Were you her type?"

Creighton opened the car door, slid in, and waited for Brisbois. "I'm every girl's type."

Brisbois gave him a sour look. "Maybe that's why you're not married."

"Naw. It's the hours we keep." He started the engine. "So, what's next? Besides six hours of uninterrupted sleep?"

Brisbois adjusted his seatbelt. "We'll have to go over the backgrounds again. Then one of us needs to go down to Montreal and check out the sleazy film studios."

"It's hard to believe Adolph doesn't have some idea of where Gerald was doing his thing."

Brisbois made to push back his hat, realized he'd lost it in the lake. He smoothed his hair instead. "I don't think Gerald was too proud of what he was doing. He probably didn't tell Adolph anything. Didn't want him coming down to his workplace because he'd forgot his lunch." He rubbed his forehead, then forced himself to stop fidgeting. He needed a new hat. "Adolph says it was about drugs and it was about a guy who hired Gerald to make porno films. At least it's a lead."

Creighton chuckled. "I wouldn't be surprised if Miss Miller invited herself to go to Montreal ."

"I don't think she's ready to give up on Mr. Harvey yet." Brisbois yawned. "We've got every detachment in the province alerted. We've got the composites out to every jurisdiction."

"We're going to have to move Adolph soon," Creighton said after a few minutes of silence. We can't leave him in that cell forever."

"I think he'd like us to."

"Are you going to tell your wife you went swimming today?"

"She'll probably be asleep when I get home." Brisbois' voice was without emotion. "Now that she has that full-time job, she can't wait up for me all night." The way she used to, he added to himself.

"One thing about being single, I don't have to worry about anybody worrying about me."

Brisbois nodded. He stared out the window, watching the moon play hide-and-seek among the drifting clouds. His wife had worried herself sick many nights, when he was delayed, or away from home for weeks. During this past year, he figured, she had worried herself out. Maybe his last escapade at the Pleasant had done that. He winced as his lower back cramped. He'd heard of such things: People removing themselves emotionally because they'd worn themselves out courting loss. Maybe it was better to live like Creighton.

He straightened and shoved his back hard against the seat. No, it wasn't. Going home to an apartment with stale air — cold in the winter because he'd left the heat down, hot in the summer because he'd left the air conditioner off — held no appeal. Creighton didn't even have dog to jump off the couch and run to him. The image reminded him of something, and he laughed.

"Something funny?" Creighton asked.

"I was just thinking about Albert. If he didn't pass gas every ten minutes, you'd think he was stuffed."

"The only time he lifts his head is when Simpson comes around. I've even seen him wag his tail for him."

"Well, Simpson's a likeable guy." Brisbois turned serious. "I believe Adolph when he says he doesn't know anything. I don't think he ever saw those two guys before."

"We'll get them. They showed their faces around pretty good. They probably figured it didn't matter since they were planning to off everybody."

"Yeah." Brisbois adjusted his seatbelt. "I'm going to Montreal."

"What about me?"

"You're going to follow up on the background checks, interview everybody again. And" — he smiled — "take a trip to the office to comb the mug shots."

"Thanks a lot, boss."

Chapter Nineteen

Creighton sat behind the desk in Rudley's office. He had been conducting interviews all day and had come close to nodding off from boredom. But when he compared a recent background check to Roy Lawson's answer to a question in an earlier interview and noted a discrepancy, he sat up and took notice. He scanned a page in his notebook, then looked across at Roy Lawson who sat opposite him.

"Why didn't you tell us you were in the funeral business, Mr. Lawson? The first time we interviewed you, you said you were an optometrist."

Roy Lawson gave Detective Creighton a sheepish look. "I didn't mean to deceive you, Detective. But people often feel uncomfortable around funeral directors." He lowered his voice. "I didn't want Pearl to know just yet."

"It would probably be better to come clean."

Lawson sighed. "I suppose you're right. But it's not as if I'd lied to her — or to you. I used to be an optometrist. Was most of my life. I got into the funeral business a few years ago. Took all the courses. Frankly, I got tired of looking into people's eyes." He lowered his voice. "Those dilated pupils sort of gave me the creeps."

Creighton gave him an incredulous look. "So you didn't come out here looking to expand your optometry business."

"No. I have a funeral home in Brockton. I'm planning to sell it and relocate to a small town. Something quiet. Where I can get to know my clients better. That's what I'm doing here. Looking into possible opportunities. Who might be thinking of retiring? Who might be willing to sell? But then I met Pearl and I got a little sidetracked. I'm sorry for my lack of candour."

"Being a funeral director is nothing to be ashamed of."

"I'm not ashamed of being a funeral director, but when I mention my profession it does tend to throw a wet blanket on the conversation." Lawson smiled. "Not to mention what it does to my romantic prospects."

Creighton raised his eyebrows. "Really?"

"I come from good stock, Detective."

Creighton rubbed his chin. "So do you need any…assistance?"

Lawson smiled. "You mean Viagra, implants, extenders?" He shook his head. "No. Fit as a fiddle in every way."

Rudley held court from the front desk. Margaret, Tiffany, Lloyd, and Tim gathered around. "So now Lawson tells Pearl he's a mortician," he said. "That explains a lot of things."

Margaret plucked a carnation from the bouquet, nipped the stem, then replaced it. "Such as?"

"His attraction to Pearl. He's scaring up business."

"Rudley." Margaret set the vase aside. "I think he genuinely likes her."

Rudley was not to be deterred. "I tell you, Margaret, those people are vultures. They'll never get their hands on me."

Margaret gave him a bewildered look. "But, Rudley, when the time comes, what are we supposed to do with you?"

"When the time comes, Margaret, you will have Lloyd dig a deep pit in the garden. He will then cover it with a heavy stone elevated planter for his tomatoes. Is that all right, Lloyd?"

Lloyd grinned. "Yes'm."

Margaret gave Lloyd a stern look. "Lloyd, it's illegal to bury a body on private property."

"No one needs to know there's a body buried anywhere, Margaret. If people wonder what's happened to me, you can tell them I died and was buried in Galt."

"What will I tell your brothers?"

"Tell them you buried me in the garden. They'll know enough to keep their mouths shut."

Margaret looked hurt. "I always assumed I'd be buried next to you."

"Not a problem, Margaret. You can dig the hole big enough for two, can't you, Lloyd?"

"Big as you want."

Rudley signed an invoice with a flourish. "The idea is appealing in every way. We won't need caskets. Lloyd could sprinkle a little quicklime around."

Margaret sighed. "I always assumed that I'd have a headstone. Something with a nice epitaph."

"Well, Margaret, you remember Ozymandias. Everything goes down to dust in the end."

"I suppose. I just never imagined I'd be remembered by a bed of beef heart tomatoes."

Rudley turned to Lloyd. "You could plant a few flowers at the corners."

"Maybe some marigolds. They keep the bugs off."

"Well, there you go."

Margaret shook her head. "I don't understand this sudden urge."

"I've been thinking about it for a while. In view of everything that's happened. Do you have any idea of what goes on in funeral homes?"

"They drain your blood off with a tube this big," said Lloyd, making a circle with his thumb and forefinger. "Then they take a mallet and turn your insides to mush so they can suck them out. Then —"

"Not to mention what goes on before," Rudley interrupted.

"What do you mean, Rudley?"

"Necrophilia."

"Surely they don't let necrophiliacs work in funeral homes."

"I doubt if they put their preferences on their resumes, Margaret."

"Oh, dear."

"I'm not saying every funeral home has an employee of that persuasion, but I'm not prepared to take a chance."

"Could be a lovely young lady, Rudley," said Tim.

"Could also be a fleshy-faced old drunk with warts like Roy," said Rudley. "So the garden it will be."

Tiffany looked distressed. "I don't suppose there'll be room for one more."

"There'll be plenty of room," Rudley said. "The only problem may be explaining where everyone went."

Margaret frowned. "Rudley, you're painting a depressing picture. All of us pushing up tomatoes."

"Oh, I wouldn't worry too much. I imagine we'll all be around for quite some time."

Creighton came up the steps. "Why all the gloomy faces?"

Margaret patted him on the arm. "We were discussing death, Detective. In view of everything that's happened."

Creighton touched his holster. "Gives you kind of a rush, doesn't it?"

"We weren't talking about dying in a hail of bullets. We were talking about passing away quietly in our golden years."

"And I get to look after the tomatoes," Lloyd said.

Creighton looked confused, then shrugged. "There's no point in obsessing about it. When it happens, it happens."

"Where's Detective Brisbois?"

"He's away. Checking out a few things." Creighton looked around. "I wanted you to know we'll be keeping two uniforms on-site until we get a handle on this thing. And we're going to hook you up to a panic button."

Rudley crossed his eyes. "I think it's a bit late for that."

Creighton ignored the jibe. "Brisbois wants it. He felt uneasy about going off and leaving you folks unprotected."

"Fine time to worry about that," Rudley said. "Not to mention the fact that the worst of it seems to happen while he's here."

"Don't worry," said Creighton. "Nothing's going to happen." He tipped his hat and left.

Rudley watched him go. "Sometimes it seems safer when it's just him."

Tiffany squeezed the handle of her broom. "He's gallant, isn't he? Chivalrous in that 1940s way. I do feel safer having him around."

"He's a regular Sam Spade," Rudley muttered.

"Oh, he's too elegant to be Sam Spade." Tiffany blushed.

"More like Remington Steele," Tim said.

Rudley waved them off. "Next thing we know, he'll be Sherlock Holmes."

Tim chuckled. "We do have the Hound of the Baskervilles."

"Albert couldn't terrorize a chipmunk if you painted him tail to nose in phosphorescent paint," Rudley murmured. He looked to where Albert lay snoring in a puddle of drool.

Chapter Twenty

Early November remained warm; the inn woke to a gentle rain. The lights, set low in the dining room, created an intimate atmosphere. Tim circulated from kitchen to dining room, bringing trays of eggs Benedict and popovers, crêpes and waffles.

"Mrs. Rudley is holding painting classes in the drawing room this morning," Tim told the Sawchucks as he unveiled the prune nappies. He whipped back into the kitchen to get the next tray and ducked his head to look out the window onto the back porch.

Norman and Geraldine Phipps-Walker were tramping off into the woods, swathed in rain gear. "I guess the P.W.s aren't interested in watercolours in autumn," he told Gregoire, who was preparing a plate of crêpes and staring moodily at the wall.

"Mrs. P.W. says there is nothing more invigorating than a walk in the autumn woods during a rainstorm," said Gregoire. "I think they are insane."

"I think they're poking around looking for evidence."

"Now everyone is an amateur detective." Gregoire sniffed. "I, for one, don't care where those terrible people are as long as they are not here." He arranged the crêpes on a plate, filled them with strawberries, and dusted them with sugar. He added tomatoes and feta cheese to the omelet in a pan, folded it, waited for a few minutes, then lifted it onto a plate. "For Miss Miller and Mr. Simpson. Don't forget the toast."

"Miss Miller still thinks Harvey orchestrated the whole thing," said Tim.

Gregoire shrugged, reached for the coffee pot, and poured himself a cup. "Miss Miller does not like to be wrong."

Tim placed the plates on a tray, hoisted it to one hand, and slipped out to the dining room.

"Thank you, Tim," said Simpson as the tray was slid onto the table.

Miss Miller smiled wanly. "Yes, thank you."

"Mrs. Rudley is leading a watercolour seminar in the drawing room," Tim said. "But, for you, Miss Miller, perhaps you'd be more interested in joining Lloyd for target practice in the coach house."

"Hand pistols?"

"Bows and arrows. Targets are bales of hay."

"Sounds like fun."

"Or you could help Mr. Bole. He's doing a finger-puppet show for the Benson sisters. *War and Peace*."

"The French on the left hand and the Russians on the right?"

"I haven't seen his show."

"Well, Elizabeth," Simpson said as Tim left, "are you up for archery?"

"I don't think my heart is in sport today."

"I know you're disappointed in the results of your investigation, but we really can't keep Mr. Harvey under surveillance in the rain."

She frowned. "We could, Edward, but I doubt if we would discover anything now that he knows we're watching him."

Simpson moistened his lips. "If I may say so, Elizabeth, there doesn't seem to be much evidence supporting your theory."

She sighed. "I hate to admit it, Edward, but I may be wrong about Mr. Harvey."

He looked at her over the rim of his coffee cup. "It's courageous of you to admit that."

She gave him a stern look. "I said may have been wrong, Edward. I'm not convinced he isn't involved in some way."

He tested his omelet and nodded with satisfaction. "Elizabeth, Mr. Devlin seems just as suspicious, although not terribly."

She tilted her head. "Do you really think so?"

He thought for a moment. "Mr. Devlin didn't turn up at the party as expected. He told the detectives his boat went on the fritz halfway out, providing himself with an alibi and an opportunity." He paused. "But I'm probably way out to sea on this."

She shook her head. "Go ahead, Edward."

He cleared his throat. "He would have been in position to help the murderer escape. He was absent for Adolph's kidnapping, giving himself the perfect alibi for that debacle. That is not to say he couldn't have aided and abetted the culprits in other ways. He was in just as good a position to gather information about the affairs around the inn as Mr. Harvey."

She narrowed her eyes. "Edward, do you seriously suspect Mr. Devlin?"

"I'm not an expert, Elizabeth, but I think the evidence against Mr. Devlin — flimsy as it is — is as good as the evidence against Mr. Harvey." He shrugged. "Except that Mr. Devlin is a dashing young man and Mr. Harvey is a bit of a toad."

She plucked a piece of toast from Edward's plate and spread jam on it. "Gregoire's homemade preserves are exquisite."

"Quite."

"You're becoming good at criminal detection, Edward."

"It is rather fun. A puzzle. However, the business of being trussed up and locked in the bowels of a boat that's being set on fire, then pitched into cold water isn't terribly appealing."

"It was a bit dicey for a while." She dabbed her lips with the serviette, then leaned forward. "Edward, let's go into Middleton today and do some touristy things. I've always wanted to visit Mrs. Merlee's tea and craft shop. We can return around dinner."

He smiled, pleased at the benign turn of events. "Sounds smashing."

"We'll be back in time for dinner, and after dinner, we've got the games tournament. I've signed us up for all the events."

"I hope they'll be having ring toss."

"They will." She gazed dreamily out the window. "That's the ticket, Edward. We'll take a day off to collect our thoughts, then tomorrow we can start afresh."

His brow furrowed. "Start what afresh, Elizabeth?"

"Our investigation."

The rain cleared, leaving a heavy mist gradually dissipated by gusts of autumn wind. Edward Simpson negotiated the damp pavement, slowing to check the street signs. "Are you sure Mrs. Rudley said the tearoom was this far over, Elizabeth?"

Miss Miller consulted her notes. "At the corner, a block up from Nesbitt's Funeral Home."

"Ghastly location for a tearoom." He slowed as an eighteen-wheeler crept out of the funeral home parking lot, blocking the street.

Miss Miller looked up and stared at the truck. She frowned. "Look at that truck, Edward."

He checked the rearview mirror. "Yes?"

"Tranquillity. It's a company that manufactures coffins."

"Yes?"

"Tranquillity is based in Montreal."

He gave her a blank look. "Yes, that's what it says on the side of the truck — Montreal."

"There's a connection, Edward." She turned to him, excited. "Who do we know who deals in coffins?"

"I don't know anyone who deals in coffins."

"Roy Lawson. He's a mortician."

"I'm confused, Elizabeth."

She grabbed him by the shoulder. "Edward, Gerald came from Montreal. Adolph came from Montreal. Roy Lawson deals in a product that originates in Montreal. Gerald was involved in pornography, which, as everybody knows, is heavily associated with the mob. Roy is in a business which is rumoured to have links to organized crime."

The truck straightened and pulled away, chuffing wisps of grey smoke. Simpson put the car in gear.

"Well, Edward, what do you think?"

They had reached the tearoom. He pulled over and turned off the ignition. "Elizabeth, there must be thousands of people who have business connections with Montreal."

"But Mr. Lawson is staying at the Pleasant. Think about it, Edward. He could be the inside man."

"I can't see Mr. Lawson as a criminal. Besides, we don't know if Mr. Lawson receives his supplies from Tranquillity. He may use a local dealer."

"It's a connection, Edward. We need to follow up all leads, no matter how tenuous."

"We?"

She smiled.

"You recall what happened last time, Elizabeth. Not to mention the time before." Seeing her unmoved, he added, "Besides, there's Mr. Harvey. We could paddle past his residence again."

She gave him a stern look. "It's not like you to be sarcastic, Edward."

"I apologize."

She got out of the car and steamed off toward the tearoom. He locked the car and followed.

"Charming place. Just as Mrs. Rudley described." He followed her to a table by the window, brushing rain droplets from his hair. He picked up the menu. "Mrs. Rudley suggested we try the strawberry scones with Devon cream. I believe she said no one could make them quite like Mrs. Merlee."

She looked at him over the menu. "Edward, you're trying to distract me."

He cleared his throat. "Yes, I am, Elizabeth, and I think that's a good thing." He paused as she gave him a steely eye. "And, I should add, virtually impossible."

The waitress approached. Miss Miller ordered scones and Earl Grey tea for two. When the waitress left, she leaned forward and said, "Edward, the Montreal connection must be explored."

"I'm sure Detective Brisbois is exploring all avenues."

She waved him off. "Oh, Edward, you know how Detective Brisbois explores things. If it were left up to him, we'd still be looking for the Northwest Passage."

"Detective Brisbois is methodical. I believe that's a good quality in an investigator."

"He takes forever to put two and two together."

"He does. But no one is in immediate danger in this case."

"What about poor Adolph? I know they've moved him to a hotel. But he's still a prisoner, unable to resume his life because someone thinks he knows something he doesn't."

"Or something he does but doesn't care to divulge." Simpson sat back as the waitress reappeared. "Thank you." He surveyed the scones. "Looks delicious." He tested his tea, then said, "I thought it was splendid of the police to plant that item in the newspaper, indicating that a witness had been taken into protective custody. Certainly increases the odds those gentlemen won't be back to plague the Pleasant. The Rudleys have had enough excitement for the season."

"They could probably tolerate a little more, Edward. They're quite hardy."

He paused. "What I'm suggesting, Elizabeth, is that we shouldn't do anything to upset the apple cart. Like investigating."

She patted him on the wrist. "Don't be a wet blanket."

"It would be prudent to let sleeping dogs lie."

She sighed, stared out the window, then brightened. "Edward, I have a plan."

He frowned.

"Just a small plan."

Gregoire and Tim were in the kitchen when Margaret came in. "What's this I hear about Tiffany breaking up with Christopher?"

Gregoire shrugged. "It's only a rumour, Margaret."

"I heard her tell Christopher she didn't think they should see each other as often," Tim said. "They happened to be coming up the back steps. I couldn't help but hear them."

"He happened to be leaning out the pantry window," Gregoire said with a sanctimonious look. "I do not regard information gained that way to be more than a rumour."

Margaret turned to Tim. "Are you sure that's what she said?"

"Yes. She also said each of them should explore other interests. She was saying the sort of things people say when what they really want to say is: 'If I see you once again in the next century, it will have been too often.'"

Margaret frowned. "I thought she seemed distracted lately."

Gregoire hefted a colander of potatoes into the sink. "I thought that might be because of all the murders taking place around here."

"It's Creighton," Tim said. "She's been casting amorous looks in his direction."

Margaret put a hand to her mouth. "Detective Creighton?"

Tim continued with relish. "It began after the boat exploded. After she saw him in my jeans."

Margaret smiled. "Well, he did look rather dashing."

"I think she's always been a bit taken with him."

"He is handsome. Tall, rather romantic with that felt hat and trench coat."

"I believe that went out of style in the forties." Gregoire sniffed. "Besides, it's unfortunate to place such weight on appearances."

Margaret looked chastened. Tim did not.

"You're quite right, Gregoire," Margaret said.

"Besides," Gregoire went on, "I think Officer Owens is still interested in Tiffany. From the way he looks at her."

Margaret nodded. "I know."

"Well, that's a fine kettle of fish," said Tim.

Gregoire placed a pepper on the cutting board and halved it with one blow. "I do not believe Detective Creighton is suitable for Tiffany. He comes across to me as a womanizer."

"I suppose he is a bit of a flirt." Margaret said.

"He strikes me as a perpetual bachelor who is only interested in his conquests."

"Well," said Margaret. "I suppose we should nip that in the bud."

Creighton took out his cellphone.

"Brisbois."

Creighton shifted the phone to the opposite ear. "You'll have to speak up, boss. It's a little noisy here."

"Where are you? In a bar?"

"I'm at the Pleasant. They're playing games in the drawing room. Snakes and ladders. Crokinole. Darts. That sort of thing."

"Anything else happened around there?"

"Not much. I'm following up on the background checks. Talking to everybody and their dog to the point of nausea. The only new thing I got is that Roy Lawson is a mortician. He didn't want to advertise the fact because he thought it might cramp his style with the ladies."

"He needs all the help he can get."

"Sure does. Miss Miller jumped on that right away. Lawson's now her prime suspect."

"You're kidding."

"No, she came back from Middleton all revved up. She noticed one of those big rigs, a Tranquillity, the ones that deliver caskets to the funeral homes."

"Yeah, I see them all the time."

"Tranquillity's based in Montreal. So she's put it all together. Lawson's a mortician. Tranquillity's out of Montreal. Gerald's from Montreal. Adolph's from Montreal."

"I get the picture. Has she got him staked out?"

"Not right now. She's too busy winning the ping-pong tournament."

"Wish her luck."

"Will do. Anything there?"

"Not much, so far. There's dozens of these little porno film shops. Some of them just making cheapies for the stag market. They close one down every now and then. Connections to drugs, prostitution, and the like. They got a kiddy porn operator last year.

We're working our way around. So far, the name Gerald Murphy doesn't ring a bell with anyone."

"What about the composites?"

"Nothing yet. Any luck on your end?"

"I've narrowed it down to a couple of thousand."

"It's a slog. We'll find them eventually."

"You're up for darts, Detective," Margaret sang out.

There was a long pause, then Brisbois said, "Watch your butt."

Chapter Twenty-one

"Congratulations, Simpson," Rudley said as Miss Miller and Simpson came down the stairs the next morning. "I hear you're champion of the dart board."

"I had a good eye last night, Mr. Rudley."

"Sorry I didn't catch your performance. I always try to say clear when darts are being thrown around. I hear Mrs. Sawchuck got one in the window frame."

Albert lifted his head as Simpson approached and wagged his tail. Simpson knelt to scratch him behind the ears.

"Albert seems more animated this morning," said Miss Miller.

Rudley nodded. "We've noticed he's taken quite a liking to Mr. Simpson."

Simpson gave Albert an affectionate pat. "I am rather good with dogs."

"Edward can have the nastiest dog eating out of his hand within minutes."

"Quite the skill."

"I believe it's a matter of not frightening them, Mr. Rudley," Simpson said.

"I think he means Albert would be more responsive if you didn't yell at him," said Margaret.

Rudley looked hurt. "I only yell because I'm always tripping over him."

"He does take up quite a lot of the lobby," said Simpson.

Margaret turned to Miss Miller. "Are you off for some exploring today?"

"We're taking a day trip to Brockton."

"Splendid. I was up there last year for an art show. Beautiful park around the river. Stone foot bridge. And if you'll be there for lunch, there's a shop near the movie theatre that specializes in exotic sandwiches and desserts. Fried pears with avocado on romaine. That sort of thing."

Albert got up, went to Simpson, and rubbed against him.

"I hope you have a lovely day," said Margaret. "But don't miss dinner. Gregoire's doing his wonderful Salmon Wellington and Baked Alaska. And it's ballroom dancing. I know how you love the samba."

Albert followed Simpson to the door, head drooping as Simpson said, "No, Albert, you must stay."

"We could take Albert with us," Miss Miller said. "He enjoys the car, doesn't he?"

"He enjoys anything he can lie down in," said Rudley.

"Albert would love a day out," said Margaret.

"We should be home late afternoon," said Miss Miller.

They took Albert down to the car. Simpson removed the leash and folded it into his pocket.

Miss Miller took the driver's seat. "Now, Edward, Mr. Lawson's funeral parlour is on McNaughton Street. I propose we get ourselves a takeout lunch and wait for the truck."

"Perhaps the truck won't be in today."

"If not, we'll go to a nearby establishment and ask when the Tranquillity truck usually comes in."

"They'll think that's an odd question."

"We'll say we're trying to find a long-lost cousin we've heard drives for Tranquillity."

"No one will tell us anything. They'll think we're chasing the chap down for money."

She tossed her head. "Then we'll just say we're obsessed with Tranquillity trucks. That we've noticed they serve several funeral homes and we're doing a survey."

He shrugged. "They'll think we're insane, Elizabeth, but at least not nefarious."

"Good."

He turned to pat Albert who was leaning over his shoulder with a wide dog smile. "Then, that's it, Elizabeth, we'll just confirm the Tranquillity truck and leave."

"Of course."

He gave her a dubious look but decided to let the matter rest.

Rudley leaned over the desk, staring gloomily across the lobby. Margaret whisked in, skirting the rug to set a fresh bowl of flowers on the mantle. She laughed.

"I'd forgotten. Albert's away for the day."

"Shows how much of an impression he makes."

Norman and Geraldine Phipps-Walker trundled up the steps into the lobby.

"You look down in the mouth, Rudley," said Norman.

"You should get outside more," said Geraldine. "Might buck you up."

"Perhaps you're right, Mrs. P.W."

"I think he misses Albert," Margaret said.

Norman looked back at the rug. "Oh, the dog's gone."

"He's not…?"

"No, Mrs. P.W. Albert went for an outing with Simpson and Miss Miller. But I'm not missing Albert."

"I'm going to stow our gear," Geraldine said. "I'll take the camera, Norman."

"Amazing camera," said Norman. "Six hundred photographs we can display in all kinds of ways, sort through at our leisure. Every birder should have one."

"Rudley could stand to have a hobby."

"I have a hobby, Margaret. It's called trying to stay sane in this asylum."

"You shouldn't take these most recent murders so hard, Rudley." Norman paused. "I hear Tiffany is no longer seeing Christopher Watkins."

"One bright spot in a dull day," said Rudley.

"I didn't think he was the right type for her."

"I didn't know you were an advisor to the lovelorn, Norman."

"Watkins didn't seem properly attentive," Norman went on. "I would think Tiffany would prefer a young man who was attentive."

"As Rudley was," Margaret beamed.

"Never pictured you as a romantic type, Rudley."

Rudley crossed his eyes. "I must say the feeling is mutual."

"When I was courting Geraldine, I brought her a plaster plaque depicting a different bird every day. Cast and painted them myself."

"I hope her quarters were substantial."

"Ours was a whirlwind courtship. I proposed when I presented her with the tenth plaque. The yellow-rumped warbler."

"That sounds very romantic," Margaret said.

"I hear she's attracted to Creighton," Norman continued. "Poor choice. Libertine."

"That does it," said Rudley. "I will not have the Pleasant turned into the Love Boat."

"One can't control these affairs of the heart, Rudley." Norman looked up as Geraldine came down the stairs. "Excuse us. Lunch time."

Rudley glowered. "What's wrong with everybody around here, Margaret? All of this interest in Tiffany's romantic life is unseemly."

"Rudley, don't be a grump." Margaret gave him a peck on the cheek. "Everyone is fond of Tiffany. They're interested in her well-being."

"Tiffany. Christopher. Creighton. Then there's the mess with Pearl."

"What mess, Rudley?"

"Billing and cooing with that old ass, Lawson."

"Oh, Rudley, they're having a wonderful time together."

"What if he marries her?"

"I think they're well suited."

"What if he wants to move in here?"

"I don't think he'd want to do that, Rudley. He has his own home."

"He's half-deaf and has warts."

"She's half-deaf too, Rudley."

He flopped down on the desk. "Maybe that's the attraction. Neither of them can hear what the other one's saying."

"You'll feel better after Music Hall. Mr. Bole is planning a tapestry of turn-of-the-century music. I'm eager to see how that turns out. And I'm working with Lloyd on his 'My Grandfather's Clock' number. His voice is coming along beautifully. Who would have guessed he had such a fine bass?"

"Not I for one."

"Our dance number will be spectacular as always."

He brightened a watt. "Yes, it will."

She tapped him on the arm. "Now cheer up, Rudley."

"All this romance going on. It makes me rather queasy."

She followed his gaze to the rug. "You do miss Albert."

"I am used to seeing him there."

"He'll be back soon. It was nice of Miss Miller and Mr. Simpson to take him for an outing. I'm sure he's having a wonderful time."

"Edward, I'm going to get lunch. Keep watch."

"Keeping watch."

He observed her walk away, then turned to Albert, who was snoring in the back seat. "I'm glad you're comfortable, Albert. I hope you realize we'll be here until that truck shows up, even if it takes until midnight."

Albert stirred and rubbed his mush against the seat cushions, leaving a sheen of drool before resuming snoring.

Simpson stretched his shoulders and settled back against the seat. Most men, he told himself, would resent spending the better part of their vacation on a stake-out. It was quite clear, however, that it was impossible to come to the Pleasant without having a murder or two take place. He sympathized with the Rudleys, who did nothing to invite such misfortune.

"You'd think it would discourage business," he said to Albert.

It didn't. The new guests seemed unaware of the extent of the mayhem. The regulars treated it as a regularly scheduled event, like Music Hall. Some of them, he suspected, enjoyed the intrigue. Elizabeth among them. She's terrifically curious, he thought, and most persistent until her curiosity is satisfied. Her determination was one of the things he found attractive about her. One of many things. She had a fine intuitive sense.

Although he didn't consider himself particularly talented in the art of detection, he was quite certain none of the staff or regulars at the Pleasant was capable of murder.

"What do you think, Albert?"

Albert answered with a muffled yorp.

He doubted if the Sawchucks had the imagination to plan a crime. The Phipps-Walkers were mainly interested in observing the passing show. He could imagine the Benson sisters poisoning someone with raspberry cordial, but he couldn't see Emma Benson up in the woods, blasting away at Lloyd's pumpkin, or Katie dumping Gerald into the lake. Louise was the most fit of the three, but even she wasn't up to much. Still, people weren't always what they seemed. Lloyd, for example. He had to admit he found Lloyd a bit sinister. Lurking about in the bushes, appearing unexpectedly at your elbow, sending your heart into a thready arrhythmia. However, he didn't think Lloyd capable of violence.

He lost his train of thought as a hearse drove into the parking lot at Lawson's.

"That's the way a hearse should look," he said to Albert. "Sleek and black. I've never cared for those bronzed things."

The hearse pulled up to the receiving doors, which were positioned behind a box hedge, effectively shielding passersby from the reality of a dead body. He mused that it would be ever so much more convenient if people simply turned to ether or a puddle of water like the Wicked Witch of the East.

The hearse didn't depress him. He didn't dwell on death. Accepted it — if it were natural and occurred in his dotage. He certainly didn't want to go with a bullet to the heart or his brains bashed out by a cudgel.

Albert was dreaming, growling low in his throat while his legs did a brisk dog paddle.

"Chasing rabbits, old boy?" Edward smiled and returned his attention to the funeral home. It was a modest, not unpleasant place, rather homey with its pink brick and sea-green awnings, its wrought-iron fence across the front, and its bay windows with Tiffany lamps.

He sighed, shifted. "I think Elizabeth has reached the end of the trail on this one," he murmured. "I don't expect much of interest to happen here." For that he was glad. The incident with the boat had been terrifying. He thought even Elizabeth had been sobered by that escapade — although she would never admit it. She seemed to assume she could get out of any mess somehow. He thought he should have tried harder to talk her out of that one, although he had to admit it was virtually impossible to talk Elizabeth out of anything once her mind was made up.

A car pulled up in front of the funeral home. A middle-aged woman and a young man got out. The woman carried a suit in a dry-cleaning bag. The man clutched a paper bag. Probably his father they just delivered in the hearse, Edward guessed.

"Who do you think did it, Albert? You probably see more and know more than anyone would imagine. Do you think either Mr. Harvey or Mr. Devlin is the culprit?"

Albert snorted.

"I agree. Neither of them has an alibi, but neither looks capable of murder." Although you can't really tell much by appearance, he knew. Most murderers don't go about foaming at the mouth. Even the two who held us at gunpoint were decidedly average. He hoped Elizabeth would eventually lose her taste for murder investigations, though he thought this unlikely. He could imagine her in her eighties turning to him and saying, 'Edward, I have a plan.'

A man in black came out the front door of the funeral home, lit a cigarette, then stood smoking and staring into space.

Simpson glanced around. A deadly still street. The tall brick houses were set close to the street, with large window boxes, heavy, drawn curtains, and larch and honeysuckle sprouting out of inlaid stone. He suspected professional couples gone all day occupied these houses, or elderly ladies who drank tea in dim parlours and took long afternoon naps.

The woman and young man came out. The man on the steps said a word to them, holding his cigarette close to his side. The grieving pair got into their car and sat for a few minutes before driving away. The man stubbed his cigarette out in a slender receptacle designed to blend in with the ironwork, then disappeared into the funeral home.

Edward jumped when Elizabeth cracked open the driver's door. Albert's nose twitched as she climbed into the seat and opened the bag.

"Chicken with sweet-and-sour pineapple in a pita pocket, fried portobello mushroom with spiced beef on rye, date squares, and coffee for us," she said. "And for Albert a dish of ground lean hamburger, rice, and" — she held up a bottle — "spring water."

Albert leaned over her shoulder, dripping saliva across the headrest.

"One minute, Albert," she said, "while I spread some serviettes." She placed the food on the serviettes in the back seat. Albert tucked in, his tail thumping. She handed Edward his share and placed the coffee in the caddy between them. "Anything to report, Edward?"

He recited his observations. "Sorry, Elizabeth, nothing from Tranquillity."

She glanced at her watch. "It's early." She took out an apple and cracked the skin with enthusiasm. "Isn't this exciting?"

He gave her a long look. "Quite."

Chapter Twenty-two

"If you need the ballroom to rehearse, feel free," Margaret said.

Mr. Bole indicated a sheaf of music. "I'd like to run through my pieces on the piano."

"Go ahead. Melba won't be setting up her harp for an hour, so you're good for at least that long."

"Doreen and I were going to run through our number," said Walter, "but Albert seems to be missing."

Rudley snapped his newspaper. "Can't you use the cat?"

Margaret gave Rudley an exasperated look. "You know she won't perform on demand." She turned to the Sawchucks. "Why don't you have Lloyd stand in until Albert returns?"

"Ditto," Rudley muttered.

Pearl came into the lobby with Roy in tow and glanced into the ballroom. "I guess we'll have to practice in the drawing room."

Margaret smiled. "I didn't know you were going to participate in Music Hall, Roy."

He gave Pearl a fond look. "Your aunt talked me into it, Margaret. Who can say no to this fine lady?"

"The more ethical bars in town."

Margaret gave Rudley a kick in the ankle.

"Roy has a fascinating voice," said Pearl. "Reminds me of Jimmy Durante. We're doing a routine called Jimmy Durante meets Sophie Tucker in the Ziegfeld Follies."

"That I'm looking forward to," said Rudley without a hint of sarcasm.

"Inka dinka doo," said Roy.

Pearl took him by the arm. "Come on, we have to get our comedic timing down."

Rudley watched them walk away. "I must say, Margaret, that does improve my opinion of him. Great vaudevillian, Jimmy Durante."

Margaret squeezed his arm. "It's such a wonderful tradition in our family. My parents. Uncle Winnie and Pearl. You and I. Now Pearl and Roy."

Rudley shrugged. "It's hard to dismiss a man with a feel for the boards." He paused. "What were the Sawchucks planning to do with Albert anyway?"

"I think he's to be Mary's little lamb."

"Appropriate."

"I've talked Mr. Harvey into coming for the night, although I don't know if he'll do a number."

"No talent?"

"He says he plays the flute, but I gather he does mostly classical pieces."

"I can see he'd be reluctant to do Bach in front of this crowd. They'd probably pitch tomatoes at him."

"Music is music, Rudley. We should consider extending our repertoire of the masters."

"Or not." Rudley couldn't contain his feet and did a quick soft shoe to the cupboard, took out a batch of invoices, and pirouetted back to the desk. "There's nothing like 'The Daring Young Man on the Flying Trapeze' to get my feet moving."

Margaret beamed. "I'm glad you've cheered up."

"You were right. The promise of Music Hall is a tonic to the soul. And" — he smiled — "Brisbois is in Montreal. Creighton hasn't left the office all morning. He's probably sacked out on the couch. If it weren't for those two flatfoots messing around the property, we could imagine we were almost normal."

"What a boring thought, Rudley."

"Quite right. Although a little boredom wouldn't be unwelcome from time to time."

Brisbois got a cup of coffee and joined his host in his cubicle. "We've harassed eleven low-budget film enterprises. How many more?"

The officer consulted his list. "Another dozen we know about."

"I think our victim got mixed up in the drug and prostitution end of it. Maybe got a little deeper into kiddie porn than was good for him."

"Which is why he never took his buddy on a take-your-kid-to-work day." The officer paused. "Do you think your guy knows more than he's telling?"

Brisbois scratched his chin. "I think Adolph's being truthful. He gave his buddy a place to stay because he felt sorry for him. I think our victim repaid him by keeping him out of the loop about what he was really up to. I gather Gerald Murphy would have done anything for money. I don't think he was a bad guy. He just liked to live beyond his means. Probably rationalized a lot."

"Lived pretty high?"

"Twenty pairs of silk jockeys."

"Sweet."

"Yeah." Brisbois flipped through the folder the officer had given him. "Snuff films." He grimaced. "I can't imagine the kind of people who want to see that stuff."

The officer sat back. "Oh, I don't know. I had a neighbour… in their family it apparently was the custom to take pictures of the deceased in their coffins. One of his boys, I swear, really got off on those pictures. Practically drooled."

"You wouldn't think a picture of grandpa full of embalming fluid would be that exciting."

The officer shrugged. "My dad said when they were kids they used to look at the full-figured ladies modelling girdles in the Sears catalogue. There are people who get off on shoes. What do I know?"

Brisbois thought for a moment. "So the people who get off on pictures of dead bodies — same types who go for the snuff films?"

The officer shook his head. "Not much. It's mostly a different demographic. The snuff-film types are evil. The other type's just kinky."

"Hmm." Brisbois nodded and checked his watch. "I've got to make a phone call."

Simpson checked his watch. "It's nearly four, Elizabeth. I doubt if we'll be seeing the truck today."

She gave him an aggrieved look.

"And it is getting dark." He smiled. "I propose we return to the Pleasant and come back another day." He glanced up the street. The windows, save for one, were dark. The lights in the funeral home glowed against the damp pavement. No one had stopped since the woman and her son. The man with the cigarette had come out twice more to have a smoke. Apart from that, they had detected no activity at the funeral home. He imagined most of the business was taking place in the basement and shuddered. "I ought to take Albert for a stroll before we head back."

A dusty white cube truck turned the corner and pulled into the parking lot at Lawson's. Miss Miller sat forward.

"Edward, look at that."

"Yes?"

"That truck."

"Indeed."

Two men got out, went to the back of the truck, and unlocked the padlock. One hopped up into the truck and released a ramp. The other went into the funeral home and returned with a trolley. Together, they rolled a coffin down, engaged the padlock, and disappeared into the back door of the funeral home.

"It's a truck delivering caskets."

"It is, Elizabeth, but I'm afraid it refutes your theory. It's not a Tranquillity."

"Where is it from?"

He squinted through the side window. "I can't tell, Elizabeth, the licence plate is rather mucked up."

Albert whimpered and scratched at the door.

Five minutes passed. The men returned with a trolley and removed a large casket and one small one. They pushed them up the ramp, closed the truck's door, and went back into the funeral home.

Simpson dipped his head. "That's a child's casket, Elizabeth. Rather sad."

She touched his arm. "You're such a sweet, sensitive man, Edward." She stared at the truck. "It may be more intriguing that Lawson doesn't use Tranquillity. Why would he use another carrier when it seems every other place uses Tranquillity?"

"Perhaps he gets a better price. Family connections. Long-standing relationship. Other preferences."

Albert whimpered again, put a leg over the seat, and pawed Simpson's shoulder.

"Elizabeth, I'd better take Albert."

"Go ahead." Her eyes were fixed on the truck. "I'll continue the surveillance."

He caught her expression. "Don't do anything risky."

She smiled. "Edward, would I ever do anything risky?"

He gave her a stern look. "Please, lock the car doors, Elizabeth." He got Albert out. Albert pushed against him, herding him toward the sidewalk. "She's reckless, impulsive, you know," he told the dog.

Albert set a brisk pace, stopping occasionally to check the foliage. A cat on a gatepost several houses up the street bristled. Albert wagged his tail and went on. Finally, he came to a utility pole, checked it out, and urinated triumphantly.

"You really are a good dog," Simpson said. "Calm, tolerant of cats. You walk well on a leash, too." Albert nuzzled his hand. "I wouldn't take it too badly that Rudley talks about you as if you were a lobby decoration, you know. I'm sure he's fond of you. If he had wanted a guard dog he would have chosen an Alsatian."

Simpson glanced at the windows as they passed. A light winked on, one he assumed had been set on a timer since he hadn't noticed any activity around the house. A heavy mist muffled and distorted the sounds, accentuating the ping of a raindrop off a downspout. He was reminded of the street he lived on in London when he was a child, which seemed civilized and ordinary. He felt homesick. He'd come to Toronto to study and wouldn't have stayed if he hadn't met Elizabeth at the Pleasant. If he'd gone home, he figured he would have met a perfectly nice young woman and be having a perfectly ordinary life, which probably would be hideously boring.

They had gone three blocks. "We'd better get back, Albert." He turned, tried to urge Albert on, then realized to his embarrassment that Albert had hunched for a bowel movement. Rummaging through his pockets to find something to retrieve the result, he looked up to see Elizabeth inspecting the licence plate of the truck. To his horror, she then opened the rear door and hoisted herself into the truck, closing the door behind her. "Damn." He strained toward the truck.

The back door of Lawson's opened. The men came out. One secured the padlock. The other climbed into the driver's seat. The man at the rear of the truck gave the door a bang with his fist, then got into the cab. The taillights pierced the gloom. Simpson took off down the street, with Albert galloping beside him.

The truck bumped over the sidewalk and backed out onto the street. As Simpson reached the car, the truck was signalling to turn right.

"I pray she disobeyed me about locking the car doors," he said to Albert, his voice shaking.

To his relief, the car door opened. The keys were in the ignition. He hurried Albert into the back seat and set out after the truck.

Chapter Twenty-three

Margaret answered the phone on the third ring. "Why, Detective, it's nice to hear from you."

"I can't raise Creighton. Do you know if he's around?"

"He said he was going to Central to look at some files and that you could reach him there. He's coming back later."

"Did he forget to charge his cellphone?"

"I believe he said something about the charger not being plugged in properly."

"Okay, I'll try him at the station. If he comes back in the meantime, tell him I'm trying to reach him." He paused. "Is Owens there?"

"I think he just came up onto the veranda. Just a moment." She placed the receiver on the desk and hurried out to the veranda. Owens was standing against the wall, staring over the lake. "Officer, Detective Brisbois is on the phone for you."

"Oh."

"In the lobby."

Owens followed her in and picked up the phone gingerly. "Owens here." He listened, brow furrowed. "Yes, I read you. Will do. Yes." He took out his notebook and jotted a number. "Got it. Two hours? All right." He hung up. "Thank you, Mrs. Rudley."

Tiffany came past the desk. Margaret pulled her aside. "Tiffany, would you get the officer a flask of coffee? It's getting a bit cold and damp out there. I would do it myself"— she glanced around furtively—"But I have something to do."

"Of course, Mrs. Rudley." Tiffany went off to the kitchen.

Margaret went to the cupboard and rummaged about. "Don't go away," she called to Owens. "Tiffany has gone to get you and your partner some coffee."

"That's very thoughtful, Mrs. Rudley."

Margaret hauled out a box, plunked it down on the desk, and began to sort through it. "She's a thoughtful young woman, our Tiffany."

Tiffany returned with a thermos of coffee and a paper bag. "Cream and sugar and two Styrofoam cups."

He flushed. "Thank you, Tiffany." He backed away, sidestepped the space normally occupied by Albert, and bumped into the door, apologizing as he squeezed out.

"Officer Owens is such a charming young man," Margaret said. "Ever so much more handsome than any of the others, don't you think?" She buried herself in a file folder, dragged out some papers, crumpled them, and tossed them into the wastepaper basket. "That sweet, open face, those soft eyes. He hasn't developed that suspicious look so many of them have."

Tiffany gave her a strange look. "Yes, Mrs. Rudley."

"Why don't you go and have your dinner, dear? Perhaps when you're finished, you could take the officers some of Gregoire's wonderful pecan pie. I'm sure they use a lot of energy, patrolling up and down, protecting us from all manner of criminal activity."

"Yes, Mrs. Rudley."

"But take your time."

Tiffany left, befuddled. Rudley came up the hallway with a cup of coffee and a club sandwich.

"Were you planning on sitting down, or should I bring you something?"

"Oh." She looked up, startled. "I'll get something later, Rudley."

He paused, watched her for a moment. "What are you doing with the files, Margaret?"

"I'm sorting them. I never imagined you had such a rat's nest in here. You should be ashamed of yourself for creating such a mess."

He put his plate on the desk, went in behind it, and retrieved one of the papers that had missed the wastepaper basket. "Margaret, this invoice just came in yesterday." He sorted through the wastepaper basket, smoothed the remaining papers, and brought them to the desk. "These are all rather recent, Margaret. If you want a rat's nest you need to dig deeper into the cupboard." He stared at the lobby rug, perplexed. "Isn't Albert back yet?"

Margaret raised her head from the folders and looked at the clock. "Oh, my, they are late. I hope they haven't had car trouble."

"They'll find a phone and call us if they're stuck. They know we'd go to get them." He patted her on the shoulder. "I'm sure they're fine."

She sighed. "Oh, you're probably right, Rudley. They're probably having such a good time they just forgot the time."

Tim leaned against the counter, waiting while Gregoire ladled marinara sauce over a serving of pasta. Tiffany stood adjacent, putting a plate together for herself, smiling.

"That's a rather provocative smile," Tim said.

Gregoire glanced at her. "Much like the cat who swallowed the mouse."

"Mrs. Rudley has a crush on Officer Owens," she said.

"No, she doesn't," said Tim. "She has a crush on Detective Brisbois."

Gregoire reached for a tea towel, ran it around the bottom of the plate, and placed it on the tray. "You are both wrong. Detective Brisbois has a crush on Margaret. Margaret does not have a crush on anyone."

"Everybody has a crush on Margaret," Tim said.

"She sent me to get him a thermos of coffee. Then she suggested he might want a piece of pie. Then she flushed and started tearing up the invoices."

Gregoire looked at Tim. Tim tittered. "I can tell you for sure, Tiffany, that Margaret does not have a crush on Officer Owens."

"I'll have you know I'm quite astute concerning affairs of the heart."

Gregoire rolled his eyes. Tim picked up the tray and waltzed off into the dining room, whistling.

Simpson panicked as he lost sight of the truck on a downtown street, then let out a sigh of relief as he caught sight of it at the corner. The car ahead of him peeled off to the right, and he found himself stopped directly behind the truck. Its signal light blinked left. He hastily engaged his turn signal. What to do? Should he jump out, grab onto the truck, hoping to get the attention of passersby? They'd probably just think he was insane and run in the opposite direction. Not that it mattered now. His chance was lost. The truck began moving again. He squeezed left behind it, sweating as the light turned red and a driver leaned on his horn. He steeled himself. Now was not the time to worry about the feelings of other motorists.

He had hoped to get a glimpse of the licence plate, planning to call the police and ask them to intercept the vehicle. But the plate was so dirty he couldn't be certain of a single number. He was sure, however, that he could make out a fleur-de-lis. That was bad news. They could be taking Elizabeth all the way to Quebec.

The truck bore no identification apart from a streak of mud he thought might conceal a registration number. He assumed it was necessary for a commercial vehicle to display such identification, although he wasn't sure. He wondered if he should try to get the attention of the truck driver. But what if Elizabeth were right? If the men were involved in criminal activity he might put her in further jeopardy by alerting them to his presence.

"I think we should stay close," he said to Albert. "If the truck stops, we'll jump out and try to get a better look at the licence plate."

Albert panted his approval, one paw on Simpson's shoulder.

The business district faded into blocks of housing. Then the truck took a left-hand turn into a narrow two-way street festooned with strip malls and down-at-the-heel storefronts. He girded himself as it passed through a yellow light. He followed, thankful no cars were bearing down on him.

It was dark now. The mist had turned to a fine rain. He turned on his windshield wipers. The strip malls fell away to scattered gas stations and coffee shops, then long stretches of low-density housing. Then a farm. He eased his foot off the accelerator as the pavement shone slick before him.

"We need a plan, Albert." He was dismayed to hear his voice quaver. He checked the side-view mirror. A thin line of cars was visible some distance behind him. Occasionally a car passed in the opposite direction, then a lumbering eighteen-wheeler that wandered close enough to the centre line to make him tremble. He'd never liked driving on the highway. He longed for the sight of a police car. He paused, brightened. That was it. As soon as he spotted a patrol car, he'd do something flagrantly illegal. Flash his high beams. Swerve as if he were drunk. That would get their attention. He would then set the officer on the truck. The plan gave him heart.

Chapter Twenty-four

Creighton thumped up the steps into the lobby.

"Have you spoken to Detective Brisbois?" Margaret greeted him. She had smoothed Rudley's invoices and returned them to the file box, brushing aside his concerns about her well-being.

He stopped short.

"He phoned an hour ago," Margaret continued. "He said to let you know he was looking for you. And that he would be back in about two hours."

"Did he say what he wanted?"

"No. But he did speak to Officer Owens."

"Okay." Creighton ducked back out and ran down the steps, shouting, "Owens."

He found Owens down by the Pines, walking slowly, his gaze sweeping the woods.

"Mrs. Rudley said Brisbois called."

Owens glanced around, then whispered Brisbois' message.

"You're kidding. Are you sure you got that right?"

"Yup."

Creighton ran a hand down his cheek. "I'll be damned."

Elmo, the driver of the truck, looked into his side-view mirror. "That friggin' car's been following us for miles."

"Are you sure?" Kenny twisted in his seat to look out the passenger's side window.

"Yeah, it ran a couple of lights." He checked the mirror again. "I'm going to pull off on the nearest side road and see if he follows."

Kenny responded by patting the holster on his right ankle.

Simpson checked the gas gauge. They had planned to fill up on the way home. The gauge now hovered near empty and the truck was turning off onto a deserted road. They had driven for what seemed like miles, although a glance at his watch showed only a few minutes had passed.

The truck slowed to forty miles an hour. Simpson eased off the gas. The car swerved as it hit a rut. He tightened his grip on the steering wheel. "I don't think this road is used often," he muttered. "Or the township council is unusually unresponsive." He wiped his lips with the back of his hand. "If you have any water left in your bowl, Albert, I think I might be persuaded to drink it."

The truck slowed, then stopped. It sat, lights blinking.

Simpson pulled to a stop. "I hope they're having motor trouble," he told Albert.

"I got what you said," Creighton said. "And I'm wondering if you've had too much to drink."

Brisbois clung to the steering wheel and pulled the phone back from his ear. "Say that again? I'm getting a lot of interference out here."

"I said I hear you."

"Okay. I'm about twenty minutes from headquarters. I want to drop by the station for a minute. I should be pulling into the Pleasant in about half an hour."

The men approached. Simpson glanced about, but he couldn't spot anything to use as a weapon. He checked to make sure the car doors were locked. The men stopped, stared at him through the windshield, then split, one going to each side of the car. The one on the driver's side motioned for him to get out. He lifted his hands off the steering wheel, smiled, shook his head. He jumped as a crash sent a shower of glass against his cheek. He put up his hand, which came away with a smear of blood. The man on the passenger's side reached through the jagged hole and unlocked the door.

"Get out."

He unlocked the driver's door and got out on wobbly legs. Albert leapt over the seat and wriggled past him

The man on the driver's side, pointed a gun at him. The other rummaged through the car, then got out, leaving the door open.

"What are you doing, following us?"

Simpson stammered. "I wasn't following you." His knees buckled as Albert pushed against him.

"Kind of a coincidence, ain't it? We saw you way back on Main Street, and you've been behind us all down the highway, and out onto this shit road."

Edward swallowed painfully. "Perhaps we have the same destination."

"I don't think so." The gunman jerked his head toward his friend. "Check him out."

The man stepped toward him. God help me, Elizabeth, Edward thought. I've done the best I could. The man rifled through his pockets, then reached inside his jacket. He could hear her say, no, you haven't, Edward. He closed his eyes and brought his knee up sharply into the man's groin. The man crumpled. Edward winced, waiting for the gunshot. Instead, he heard a low growl and a surprised scream. He turned to see Albert on top of the second man, teeth bared. In the headlights he saw the gun a hand away from Albert's victim.

He reached for the gun. The man punched Albert in the head. Albert responded by sinking his teeth into the man's lower lip.

Simpson gripped the gun. "Albert, come here. Now." He edged toward the truck, keeping the gun leveled. The first man continued to writhe on the ground. He glanced into the truck and almost fainted with relief when he saw the keys in the ignition.

He opened the door and hurried Albert into the passenger's seat. The man Albert had savaged started toward them, screaming.

Edward jumped in, slammed the door, and punched the locks down. "All right, Albert," he whispered, "I've never driven one of these, but it can't be that difficult." He put the truck in first and it lurched forward. In the mirror, he saw the man break off the pursuit and run for the car. He fumbled the truck into second gear.

The car was gaining on them, then it stopped.

Simpson wiped his forehead. "Albert, I believe they've run out of gas."

"It's almost six-thirty, Rudley." Margaret picked up the phone. "I'm calling the police."

Rudley peered out the window.

"It isn't like Miss Miller and Mr. Simpson to be delayed," she added.

"It is like them to be delayed, but usually it's because they're in some kind of mess." He pointed to the phone. "Call the police." He said the last word as if it strangled him. "Call them."

Brisbois pulled into the service station and surveyed the scene before getting out of the car. A white cube truck sat just beyond the pumps. A uniformed officer was speaking to a youngster in coveralls. A large furry dog lay tethered to the bike rack. A man who looked suspiciously like Edward Simpson sat in the back of the patrol car. Brisbois shook his head, got out of the car, approached the officer, and showed his identification.

The officer tipped his hat. "Didn't expect they'd send you out here, Detective."

"I was at the station when the call came in." He gestured toward the truck. "What's going on? These back roads are jumping tonight."

"That guy" — the officer pointed toward the cruiser — "pulled in here in that truck. Asked the proprietor to call the police. Claims" — he checked his notes, shook his head — "now let me read this back to you, word for word. This is about the weirdest story I've heard in a long time."

Brisbois listened, suppressing a smile. "Are you telling me by any chance that a certain Miss Miller's locked in the back of that truck?"

"Well," the officer began, shooting Brisbois a puzzled glance, "he asked the kid"—he indicated the attendant—"for a pair of bolt cutters to break the padlock. The kid was justifiably reluctant. Something about her trying to kick the door down. He thought it best to wait until help arrived. I thought the same thing." He gestured toward the cruiser. "This gentleman—Simpson—mentioned your name. I didn't pass that on to dispatch, so I was surprised when you showed up. I figured you must be telepathic."

Brisbois gestured vaguely. "I heard the names floating around." He pointed toward Albert. "I see you arrested the dog, too."

"You know the dog?"

"Yes, but I think it's the first time I've seen him awake." He glanced toward the truck. "Open it up. It might be wise if I were the first person she sees."

"Is she dangerous?"

"Moderately."

The officer nodded to the attendant who left and returned with a pair of bolt cutters. At Brisbois' nod, he snapped the padlock and stepped back. Brisbois stepped up to the door. "Miss Miller, it's Brisbois. You can come out now."

There was a pause, then the door opened. Brisbois offered a hand. Elizabeth smiled sweetly in acceptance and stepped down.

"So tell me your story, Miss Miller."

She swept dust from her sleeve. "We were on a stake-out at Lawson's funeral home in Brockton. A white truck pulled up. We observed two men unloading things and carrying them into the funeral home."

"Things?"

"Coffins."

"Sounds suspicious so far."

Miss Miller indulged his skeptical remark. "While Edward was walking Albert, I decided to check the truck."

"And?"

"It was empty. I heard the men returning so I shrank back against the wall. I thought at worst I'd have to wait until they got into the cab before hopping out. As it turned out, they not only closed the door but padlocked it."

"Uh huh."

"Unfortunately, I wasn't privy to the details of what went on after that. I do remember a long drive, the truck stopping, a dog barking, a few shrieks. The next thing I knew, the truck started up again and we arrived here after a rather horrendous ride."

"I guess Simpson isn't used to driving a truck."

She ignored that. "The truck stopped. I heard Edward's voice. Then an argument ensued in which these gentlemen" — she indicated the officer and the attendant — "refused to release me."

"That was prudent, Miss Miller. They couldn't be sure what was going on." He smiled. "Not knowing you as I do." He raised his brows. "I think what you're really peeved about is being locked in the truck while all the action was taking place."

She gave him a disparaging look over her glasses. "What now, Detective?"

He tipped his hat back. "I think we should start by releasing Simpson and Albert and get you back to the inn. Once you've had a chance to recover, I'll take a full statement."

"I suppose our car is long gone," Miss Miller said as they started back toward the inn.

Brisbois smiled. "As a matter of fact, no."

"You found it?"

"One of our patrolman did. As I was saying to the officer back there, it's been a wild night in our neck of the woods. It seems two men tried to siphon gas from a Jeep parked in front of a hunting shack. A pack of good old boys with shotguns came barrelling out. They held the gas thieves and called us on a cellphone. The men gave the officer a story about running out of gas and not knowing anybody was home. Planned to borrow the gas and leave some money and a note. That sort of thing. When the officer checked the registration it didn't match up with their ID. They figured car theft." He glanced into the rearview mirror where Simpson sat with Albert. "How does it feel to be a hero, Simpson?"

"Actually, I think Albert's the hero, Detective. We wouldn't have escaped without him."

"Would you have fired that gun if you had had to?"

There was a pause. "I don't think I could have hit the broad side of a barn door, Detective. Fortunately, they didn't know that."

Brisbois shook his head.

Brisbois let his passengers out at the back door. "Go in quietly. Try not to attract too much attention for the time being."

Miss Miller smiled. "I think we can manage that."

Brisbois waited until they had gone inside, then pulled around to the front. Creighton was waiting on the veranda.

"Everything under control?"

"Yup."

"Okay, let's do it."

"They're in the ballroom."

Brisbois and Creighton entered the ballroom. Tiffany was on stage with Lloyd, accompanying him on the piano. Mr. Bole, the Sawchucks, and the Phipps-Walkers watched from the floor. Mr. Harvey sat beside Margaret holding a flute while she reviewed a piece of sheet music. Pearl and Roy sat at the next table. Pearl was laughing and shuffling cards.

Brisbois crossed the floor and stopped in front of Margaret and Harvey. "Margaret."

Margaret gave him a questioning look. "Detective?"

"Sorry to disturb your rehearsal," he whispered in her ear.

She frowned and looked to Mr. Harvey.

Brisbois leaned toward the next table and tapped Roy on the shoulder. "Mr. Lawson, if you'll come with me…"

Chapter Twenty-five

Brisbois filled his cup from the carafe before responding to Miss Miller's question. "When we searched the funeral home, we found an appreciable amount of cocaine and Ecstasy in that baby coffin."

They were in the dining room at the Pleasant. Miss Miller turned to Simpson. "I knew he was up to no good."

Simpson shook his head. "I must say, Mr. Lawson seems an unlikely drug dealer."

Brisbois shrugged. "He didn't want to be a drug dealer. But they had something on him."

Miss Miller leaned forward. "Mr. Lawson was quite talkative, then."

"He's trying to reduce his sentence."

She tilted her head. "I don't suppose you could tell us what he had to say."

He hesitated, then relented. "Our Mr. Lawson got himself into a compromising situation. He was quite the consumer of pornography. He spent a lot of time in Montreal. Got to know Marcel Dupré — drug dealer, porn distributor. Roy decided he'd like to star in his own film, something he could take home and enjoy over and over. His costars were young girls — fourteen, fifteen mainly."

"Not the sort of film likely to win any Oscars."

"No. But Dupré kept a copy. So when he came calling for a favour, Roy felt he had to oblige."

"He became a snitch."

"He prefers to say he was gathering information. He watched and listened. Wheedled what he could out of Aunt Pearl."

Miss Miller grimaced. "Which wasn't difficult, given that she was smitten with him."

Brisbois shrugged. "And half-potted most of the time. Anyway, he got things right about Gerald. Gregoire's comings and goings and so forth. But he messed up pretty thoroughly on Adolph. First, he got the location wrong." He paused. "Our boys — Serge Michaud and Mitch Flanagan, by the way — their first impulse was to snatch Adolph from the Oaks and do him in in some discreet locale. But the cottage was too exposed. Lawson told them about the Halloween party and about the incident the year before where somebody shot up the pumpkin patch. Our boys saw that as a good distraction. They positioned themselves in the woods and waited."

"And shot up the place, Rambo-style."

"Yes. And you know how that worked out, Miss Miller." Brisbois paused to sample his coffee. "Anyway, Lawson finally figured out where Adolph was. Serge and Mitch tried to keep it simple this time. They snatched him from the High Birches and got to hell out of there."

"Because Mr. Lawson had informed them there were police officers on the premises."

"Right."

She frowned. "What I don't understand is why didn't they simply dump Adolph in the middle of the lake and make their getaway?"

"They wanted to get him out of sight and get him to a place where they could interrogate him, undisturbed."

"But why Harvey's?" she persisted.

"Because Lawson advised them it was secluded and that Mr. Harvey posed no threat and had a big boat. They figured they could stuff Harvey and Adolph into the boat, take them upstream, and make it look as if somebody got careless with the gasoline." He smiled. "Mr. Lawson also picked up on the fact you saw Mr. Harvey as a suspect,

Miss Miller. He thought using Mr. Harvey would further confuse the investigation."

Simpson spoke up. "I think it would have been more straightforward to shoot us on the spot."

Brisbois made an I-agree gesture with his right hand. "They didn't want to make it look like a gangland execution. They didn't count on your resourcefulness, Miss Miller. Letting that canoe float was a lifesaver."

She looked disappointed. "Our diminutive Mr. Lawson was behind the entire escapade."

Brisbois nodded. "Lawson was helpful in all sorts of ways. He gathered information. He let Serge and Mitch use his house outside of Brockton as a staging area. He let them know Devlin was out of town. They stashed their car behind his place. The plan was to scuttle the outboard, get rid of their stuff, and make a clean getaway."

"Why were they so eager to get rid of their jackets and caps?"

"That gear might have made them look like good old boys around here, but it was kind of loud for guys on the lam."

"Do you think Mitch and Serge will ever be apprehended?"

Brisbois sat back. "As a matter of fact, Mr. Simpson, they were picked up outside of Shawinigan last night. One of the patrolmen tried to pull them over. They decided to outrun him. He called ahead and set up a roadblock. They were hauled into the station where someone recognized them from our composite."

"Obviously, our descriptions were good."

"They were, Miss Miller." Brisbois smiled. "The funny thing is the only reason the officer pulled them over was to tell them one of their rear wheels was wobbling."

Miss Miller considered this. "So you've rounded up all the bad guys."

"Pretty much. Everybody squealed on cue."

"Then Adolph is safe to resume his life," Simpson said.

"I think he's going to be okay."

"It seems those gangsters would have been better advised to have left Gerald and Adolph alone," Simpson said.

"I'm sure they'd agree with you about now."

Miss Miller sighed. "I'm sorry about Gerald. And I'm sorry about Aunt Pearl. She must be devastated."

Rudley leaned over the desk and watched as Pearl came down the stairs. She stopped in front of the desk.

"I'm sorry things didn't work out, Pearl."

She shrugged. "Oh, it's all right, Rudley. It was a gas while it lasted. He played a great game of cribbage, had a pretty good sense of humour, and was a dreamy dancer and a snappy dresser." She paused. "He was a hell of a lot of fun. But he was a lot more fun when I thought he was an optometrist. After I found out he was a mortician, you might say the bloom was off the rose."

"Then it was all for the best."

She patted his cheek. "He's not the only fish in the lake. I think I'll have Tim fix me an aperitif."

Margaret came in with Albert. "Sit, Albert, while I remove your leash."

Albert obliged, then ran in behind the desk and offered Rudley a paw.

"Being a hero has certainly increased his intellectual capacity, Margaret."

"He always had it in him, Rudley. He just needed a little recognition."

Brisbois came out of the dining room. "Margaret, Rudley, I think we can return your office to you."

"That's gracious of you."

"I may need to come back for some follow-up interviews, of course."

Rudley crossed his eyes.

"Are you going to take some time away, Detective?" Margaret asked. "Now that the case has been solved?"

He sighed. "I may be able to scrounge a few days."

"Why don't you use those few days to take your wife for a nice trip?"

He paused. "She's working full-time now, Margaret. I don't know if she could take the time."

"I'm sure she would if you asked."

He gave her a long look, then smiled. "You may be right." He tipped his hat. "Until next time."

"Margaret," — Rudley put an arm around her — "peace reigns. At last."

"Not entirely, Rudley." She sighed. "It seems Tiffany has a date with Officer Owens' partner. She found out he writes poetry and plays the clarinet."

"That brainless Semple? The one who got his foot stuck in a hole?"

"I'm afraid so."

"Well, damn to hell. Does that mean we'll have him and his big flat feet hanging around?"

"I wouldn't put it that way, Rudley."

"Couldn't you teach Owens to paint or play something?"

"I'm afraid the arts aren't part of his repertoire."

Rudley digested this. "Apart from your disappointment as a matchmaker, everything else worked out."

She tapped him on the arm. "That nice Mr. Corsi…"

"Slipped out without paying his bill?"

"Oh, no. He says he wants to make a film about us."

He thought for a moment. "No one would believe it, Margaret."

She sighed. "You're probably right."

Acknowledgments

Every life is a tapestry of all the lives that have touched it. Mine has been touched by hundreds of nurses and thousands of patients, each of whom has left their imprint. I particularly remember the first four patients placed in my care. Although forty-five years have passed, I remember their faces, their names, and the rooms they were in. I even remember their bathrobes.

I would like to acknowledge the people who held a special place in my life when I was a kid:

My cousins Elaine Young and Arnold Alguire — the kids I grew up with.

My aunt Louise Moore — she made the best cherry cake ever.

My aunt Marie Robertson — she made going to funerals fun.

The kind lady at the United Church Sunday School picnic — she saved the last piece of chocolate pie for the little kid who could barely see over the table.

And the people who hold a special place in my life now that I'm a big kid:

Janice Deakin and Sue Croswell — always generous and supportive.

Julie Fox, who is a good egg.

In closing, I would like to thank Karen Haughian, publisher of Signature Editions, for making the Rudley series possible. I would also like to thank my editor Doug Whiteway for his diligent efforts to make *The Pumpkin Murders* the best it can be.

About the Author

Judith Alguire's previous novels include *Pleasantly Dead*, the first of the Rudley Mysteries, as well as *All Out* and *Iced*, both of which explored the complex relationships of sportswomen on and off the playing field. Her short stories, articles and essays have also appeared in such publications as *The Malahat Review* and *Harrowsmith*, and she is a past member of the editorial board of the *Kingston Whig-Standard*. A graduate of Queen's University, she currently works as a visiting nurse in the Kingston area.